To k
MERRY C...

MW01277875

69 Shades of Green

7 Days in Heaven

John Westley

69 Shades of Green
is copyright John Westley
All rights reserved

Published by Thornhill Press
www.thornhillpress.com

Contents

John Westley

A man and his girlfriend decide to tie the knot. Soon after their wedding his wife says, "Now that we're married I think it's time you gave up golf. Do you think you could sell your clubs?" The man looks at her and says,

"Boy. You're beginning to sound like my ex-wife."

"I didn't know you were married before!" she exclaims.

The man again looked at her and replied, "I wasn't."

Chapter ~~69~~ 1

There are some things I know a lot about, and much I know little about. And a few things I thought I knew a lot about, and it turned out I knew little. I thought I knew a lot about golf. And women.

I was aware I knew little about Canada. Most Americans do not know much about Canada, perhaps because it is so far away. I was born and raised in Portland, Oregon. One of the first things I learned while in Canada was that Americans never come from just a city. They come from a city *and* a state. A Canadian might be from Toronto, an Australian from Melbourne, a frog from Paris, and a Brit from London. But I am not from Portland; I am from Portland, Oregon.

While I cannot call myself an extensive traveler, I have traveled a bit playing professional golf. I have been to Mexico, parts of Asia, South Africa, down under to Australia, but never to Canada. Hell, I had never even been to Seattle. Seattle, Washington, that is. Despite not having been there previously, my connection to Canada was not completely non-existent. I love NHL hockey, consider myself a distant disciple of Moe Norman and… I flew Air Canada once.

The Air Canada flight sticks in my mind because I was flying back from the PGA Trade Show in Orlando, Florida. While at the show I had been given a new sand wedge to try out, and was bringing it home with me. I did not have my golf bag with me (only because United lost it – that is another story) and obviously did not want to check the sand wedge as luggage. Being a shorter club I knew it would fit in the overhead compartment so I brought it as carry-on baggage. I checked in, got all the way through security, waited in the waiting room, got called to board, walked all the way down the jetway and then was not permitted to board the plane because... my sand wedge did not have a special security clearance tag.

"A special *what?*" I asked.

"Your golf club needs a special tag, as it could be considered a weapon," the otherwise cute flight attendant told me.

"A weapon?" I asked incredulously. "You mean like the scientists at Control turned it into a machine gun?"

"You could attack the crew with it. It's no big deal, you just have to go back to check-in and get a red clearance tag."

If it was not so funny I would have been terribly mad. "But check-in is back at the other end of the airport. I could do two rides at Disney on the way!"

"I'm sorry sir, you need the tag."

"And the tag will render the club harmless as a weapon?"

The flight attendant just smiled impatiently back at me. Cute smile as I recall, but I was not seeing it at that particular moment. So, I ran back to check-in, got the silly tag, tore back to the gate, jetted down the jetway, boarded the plane and continued on, now aware that golf club control was the true key to Canada's reputation as a violence-free nation.

***

Fast forward to the beginning of this story, which begins on a boat, in Canada. I had just been as far west as you can go in the true north strong and free, in a place called Tofino on the west coast of Vancouver Island, which itself is west of Vancouver, British Columbia. Tofino is a bit of an anomaly in terms of Canadian geography – at least in how we foreigners perceive it. Tofino is known not for its skiing, not for its snowshoeing, but for its surfing. Yes, surfing. Typically dense rainforest suddenly gives way to a vast expanse of sand – not inappropriately called *Long Beach* – with surf waves that, while in no way rivaling those of Hawaii, or even California, possess a charm and mystique I had never seen before. Yes, I gave it a go. Who knew if I would experience something like this ever again? It was early Canadian summer and while you could burn your face sitting on the beach, the air was cold and the

Pacific Ocean colder. A wetsuit was not an option.

So why was a golf pro from Portland (Oregon) surfing in Tofino, Canada? I guess you could say I was finding my game. Although that is not actually what this story is about. Finding my game was just a catalyst to finding something greater. Much greater. I had read some articles, and subsequently some books, written by a reclusive Canadian teaching professional who resided on the west coast of Vancouver Island. My game had plateaud and I had reached a crossroads: do something radical and make a real go at tournament golf, or give up the dream and join my dad's trucking firm. Another option might have been teaching, but the thought of teaching such a difficult game to hackers was abhorrent to me. And, for some reason, it does seem the only good golf teachers are the eccentric types who teach in a field adjacent to rugged surf beaches, and that was not me. The ones who hang out at driving ranges, or wear their sunglasses backwards at country clubs, are in my opinion a complete waste of time. The thought of becoming one of those was even more abhorrent than of the actual teaching.

Now, I am not a flake. I did not drive all the way to the extreme west coast of Canada with a fanciful notion some golf whisperer was going to brew some herbal Canadian ale that, once consumed, would cure all that ailed my swing. His writings were deeply practical, focused on a root and not symptoms, and while in many instances they defied tradition in golf they did not defy logic. The logic was overwhelming. But so was my muscle memory. Re-writing that memory was not going to be easy, no matter how well-founded the logic. I had decided to give everything I had to tournament golf, so committing a month to working with a Canadian golf guru seemed the minimum effort required; not overkill. This is not to say there was no risk. This guy could have turned out to be some granola-eating, snowball-throwing nut with good health insurance. But nothing good comes without risk and this turned out to be a risk worth taking. I am a ten-year golf pro who played another ten years of junior/amateur golf, and I learned more in one month with this guru than I had the rest of my golf career. The instruction was fairly simple; his bigger task was getting me to let go of a lifetime of myths and misnomers.

It was quite humbling spending two weeks arguing swing theories with nothing to back me up. Even I began to tire of hearing my own voice saying things like, *"It's always been that way,"* or *"But I was always told…"* or *"Everyone knows you have to do that"*. When he would ask me, politely, "Yes, but *why* would you do that?" I never had an answer. Let alone a good one. So my month with the guru was basically broken down into two weeks of arguing followed by two weeks of really productive practice. I did not learn any new skills, just a new way of looking at the mechanics of the golf swing and the ability to self-correct in the future. And yes, there was some muscle memory re-writing involved, but not nearly as much as anticipated, and what I had to memorize was relatively simple given my new knowledge. Nonetheless, it was not lost on me that had I argued so stubbornly for two days - instead of two weeks - it would have given me more time to practice. And surf.

It was with a sense of forlorn that I departed Camp Guru and began the very windy single lane journey that would take me to the ferry terminal in Nanaimo, and my discovery of another Canadian secret, the decadent dessert known as the Nanaimo Bar. I loaded up with the aforementioned dessert and a plethora of sandwiches as I had been warned about the food on the ferry. Unfortunately no one had warned me about the coffee or the fact absolutely zero alcohol would be available on board.

It was a huge ferry, holding 370 cars and adorned by monumental murals depicting Winter Olympic athletes, a holdover from Vancouver's hosting of the Games in 2010. I accidentally found myself the best seat on the ferry, across from the women's washrooms.

Tofino had certainly given me no indication of how incredibly beautiful Vancouver women were. I cannot vouch for what percentage of the women I saw were in fact from Vancouver, as this was the beginning of tourist season and I was on a vessel that transported tourists, but nonetheless my head was spinning. And talk about eclectic! From well dressed with the finest labels to interestingly dressed with the tightest labels. For every woman with form fitting yoga gear there was another with painted on jeans, and yet another with more tattoos than clothing. Blondes seemed to abound, to the degree I began leaning forward to hear if any were speaking Swedish. Upon reflection, I would have to say there were just as many dark haired beauties, buoyed no doubt by the significant Asian population in that part of the world.

I found myself at peace, for the first time in a long while. I had wondered many a time if I would ever feel inner peace again; I certainly could never have predicted it would be on a Canadian ferry sitting across from the women's washroom. Golf - and my obsession with my swing problems - had preoccupied my mind for so long that I think I had completely forgotten what it was like to fantasize about being with a soft, exotic, sexy woman again. Oh I had managed to lust after women during my era of golf swing woes, even sleep with a couple. But now my mind was wandering to more romantic scenarios. Hot, yes, but with a romantic element I had forgotten I was capable of. Maybe did not even know I was capable of. My thoughts went from, *"I'd like to do that one,"* to *"I wonder what a weekend in a remote cabin would be like with her?"* I had been told the view on the journey from Vancouver Island to the Vancouver mainland was a good one, but I had thought I would need to at least look out the window. Finally, a large woman appeared, with big hair and an even bigger backside all squeezed into lululemon yoga pants, allowing me to switch my mind back to golf for a moment.

For once I was thinking forward, to the adventures that lay ahead for me, rather than back, to disappointments. I think part of my problem in the past was not just poor play, but playing poorly and not having a clue why. It was yet to be proven, but somehow I now had a sense that while it was undeniable there would be future poor shots, poor holes, even poor rounds, I would be able to deal with it all much better because I would know why, and be able to go away and work on the issue with a sense of understanding.

I was also looking forward to my travels. As I said, I have traveled a bit, and was astounded to find a brand new world in a country so close, and that I had hitherto ignored. My mind wandered, far from lululemon lady and to the highway that lay ahead enroute to a place called Heaven, BC. It was now Friday evening, and I was entered to Monday-qualify for the Husky Open, an event on the Canadian Tour. I would spend one night in the metropolis of Vancouver, drive all day Saturday, practice Sunday, and give it my best shot on Monday. I would need to finish in the top three on Monday to have a place in the field come Thursday. I was excited. My excitement dissipated momentarily when lululady re-emerged from the washroom, with a piece of string dangling from her pants. I turned and looked out the window. They were right, the scenery outside was fabulous.

John Westley

Chapter ~~69~~ 2

Vancouver was a bit of a shocker in terms of hotels. Prices, that is. You can stay in my hometown of Beaverton (near Portland) for under fifty bucks *and* get coffee and donuts in the morning. In Vancouver I gravitated toward what seemed to be lesser hotels thinking they would be more in my price range. They were not. Not even close. $120 per night for a dive. Even if I wanted to stay there, that was way out of my league. And I was in the minor leagues, remember. People who Monday-qualify on any of the mini-tours cannot afford hundred dollar a night accommodations. But I lucked out.

A summer fireworks festival was just beginning as I was traversing what is known as the North Shore of Vancouver. I drove up what basically is a mountain, to a posh neighborhood aptly named the British Properties. There I was able to park and watch the fireworks. The night was warm, and the view truly was incredible from my perch above. Looking down I could see an enormous suspension bridge connecting the north shore to downtown, from which the fireworks emanated. Water matched or exceeded land in terms of viewable coverage. Marine activity was unparalleled as crafts varying from sailboats to two giant cruise liners and everything in between jockeyed for position to watch the evening's show in the sky. I still had sandwiches and now some beer to complement them, so I sat quite happily eating, drinking, and watching the explosions of color down below.

By the time the show was over I was quite sleepy and not keen to join the throng scurrying for home. It is always the same at a fireworks show: over the course of a couple of hours thousands show up to view it, and over the course of a few minutes those same thousands dart for their cars and try to scram. The bottom line was I had nowhere to scram to. I grabbed a sleeping bag from the trunk, which I used to lie on rather than in, and wondered if I would be safe sleeping in the car overnight. I was not worried about my safety, per se, but being such a rich neighborhood wondered how long it would be before a patrol car would come by and usher me along. I never found out.

The sun rises early in this part of the world, at this time of year. I have never been the biggest sunrise kind of person, but on this particular morning I could see suddenly what all the fuss was about. I could even see the irony that lay in the fact that mere hours earlier thousands had assembled to watch twenty minutes of pyrotechnics in the sky, while now mother nature was putting on a far more spectacular show in that same sky and there was no one but me in attendance. Oh, and one jogger – who actually fit into her lululemon outfit. Incredible. Probably ten years older than I am, but fitter and extremely well put together fashion-wise. And that was just for her morning jog. I began to wonder which of these multi-million dollar homes she was running from, or to. Was she married to a doctor? Or, up at this hour, perhaps she was the doctor? For sure I could not go to a doctor that good looking – for reasons I need not explain.

So things were going perfectly. I had found myself economical accommodations with a built-in light show, woke to an incredible sight, and a very nice sunrise as well. Despite it being five in the morning I did not feel tired and saw this as an invitation to get on the highway early and start my drive to Heaven, British Columbia. A gift from my big sister, I had been given a GPS which was coming in incredibly handy. According to it, I had about nine of hours of driving ahead of me. With this early start, I could do the lions' share of the drive before lunch, take my time eating, and then coast into Heaven.

Describing the drive from the coast into the interior of British Columbia could fill a book, and it was not my intent to write a travelogue. But it was mind blowing; nothing I had ever seen before. Mountains, valleys, hills, lush forests turning into desert. I felt like I was traveling through several countries, not one state. Sorry, states are called provinces in Canada. They are a provincial lot.

It only seemed fitting, as I was headed to Heaven, that I stop for lunch in Hope. This was much sooner than planned, but the further east I headed the smaller and the older the highway became, and thus slower. That was when I learned that GPS's are made by the same people who predict the weather. The original prediction really means nothing. The trick is to keep re-calibrating and change the prediction frequently based on current conditions, until you reach the point where if you stick your hand out the window, and it gets wet, you can predict it is raining. But for once in my life I was not panicked. I had, and had allowed for, an all day drive to get to my destination and somehow it just made good sense to stop in Hope for lunch, before getting to Heaven for dinner.

I was hungry, too. And damn me if I did not nearly walk into a Subway for another sandwich. I literally stopped in the middle of the road (not a busy one) and contemplated just how American I was. I remembered a trip to Cancun and being astounded at the enormous line-up of my fellow countrymen waiting to get into... a Hard Rock Café. Amazing local Mexican food in abundance all around and there was a line-up at the Hard Rock. I was doing the same thing. Sort of. But I stopped myself! I looked around and saw what appeared to be a quaint Canadian small town restaurant attached to a small town grocery store three doors down from the Subway. That was where I would have my lunch this day.

I walked through the wood-framed screen door and was immediately greeted by the maitre d'. She was short, Chinese, and maybe nine years old. She took me to my table, offered me a menu, poured me a glass of water, and then yelled something in Chinese to her parents in the back. *Almost* everything on the menu was Chinese food, but for a "hamberger" (sic) "spagheti" (also sic) and this was the strange one: "Caesar salad". Most American restaurants spell Caesar wrong and in this restaurant that was the only thing spelled correctly. I ended up deciding on the sweet and sour chicken balls. I was in Canada, and I'd be damned if I did not eat what the locals ate.

Everything I ate was brought to my table by the nine year old little girl, while who was presumably her mother remained in the kitchen to yell at whom was presumably the father. The mother would yell, then peep out the little window from the back kitchen and smile broadly as if she wanted me to know she had all her teeth. I know this will sound silly, but I asked the little girl if she knew how much further it was to Heaven. She thought it was silly, too.

"Heaven?" she asked with a laugh.

"Yes I want to go to Heaven."

"Be good boy," she responded.

69 Shades of Green: 7 Days in Heaven

First I felt silly asking a nine year old for directions, now I realized how silly *what* I was asking, sounded. "No, no, I am driving to Heaven. To the *town* of Heaven. Heaven, British Columbia." The little girl stared blankly back at me, then turned and ran to the kitchen. A short moment later, her mother with all the teeth came out to my table for the first time.

"You want to go to Heaven?" she asked. I nodded. She pointed upward.

"No, the town of Heaven," I clarified. It is east of here; I just want to know how many hours. Or miles?" The mother looked at me, and laughed.

"Oh, miles. You are funny mister." She turned and yelled something in Chinese back to her husband who was sheepishly peering through the opening from the kitchen. The second she turned in his direction he ducked, as if to avoid being seen but she kept on yelling. I do not think she was asking where Heaven was. But maybe she was, because the husband (without reappearing) yelled something back. She turned to me again. "No Heaven. We don't know Heaven. We don't know where it is. We not know it," she told me.

"You don't know Heaven?" I asked. Then it dawned on me they may not have lived here long. "How long have you lived here?"

"25 years," she answered proudly. There went that theory. She walked a few steps, to another table, and asked an old man seated there all by himself.

"You know Heaven?" she asked of him.

"What?" he replied. "You mean the town of Heaven?"

"Yes!" she replied emphatically.

"Oh hell, Heaven is about four hours east of here." He somehow knew to direct this at me. "But blink and you'll miss it. It might be the smallest town in B.C."

"You're kidding," I said.

"Nope, not at all. It was originally to be a Mormon community, but then they all headed to Bountiful. Ain't much there but a post office and a golf course," he added.

"So there is a golf course?" I asked with childish enthusiasm.

"I hear it's a gem; one of the best in B.C. Don't care much for golf myself, though I might change my mind when I get old," said the man eating the senior special.

And so it was game on. My tummy full of Canadian grub I returned to my car prepared to drive for four hours - the equivalent of an average game of golf. I was full of hope and headed to Heaven. Life was good.

Chapter ~~69~~ 3

Life had not always been good. Like many (or all) of us my life had its ups and downs. It is probably more accurate to say my life had been neutral before. A flat line, so to speak. But there is nothing like a big dip down to make what preceded, as boring as it may have been, seem like an up. The thing I learned is that I was immensely inexperienced at handling downs. Some people truly do have significant ups and downs in their lives, and to their credit they become quite skilled – strong – at dealing with their challenges. People like me who have relatively uneventful lives spiral more, I think, when adversity strikes.

My adversity was 5'5" and drank like a fish. The night we met she drank a lot and I thought it was cool. Dumb guy thing, thought it was cool a chick could match me beer for beer. Stupid, I know. The next few times we went out she only drank a beer or two, and that seemed perfectly normal. And reasonable. But for those who are attending A.A. it is not so reasonable. I thought she was going to art class Tuesday nights, but that was meeting night. From what I understood she showed up to meetings but did not participate, which kind of flew in the face of the whole A.A. credo as I understood it. By showing up and not participating she could claim she was doing something proactive about her problem, while not really having to take any responsibility for getting better. And so she got worse. The only part that got better was the sex, until that got worse too.

Sex for her was as much an escape as the drinking was. A little alcohol, mixed with a high libido and nothing else to do can lead to some pretty great sex. And when you are having pretty great sex you can dupe yourself into thinking nothing is wrong. In fact, I really believed things in general were pretty great. However, in our case her drinking led to more drinking and more drinking led to less sex. And lazy sex. Or no sex at all. Lack of sex does not really qualify as one of life's downs (although one could argue that great sex does qualify as one of life's ups) but the fallout from alcoholism sure does. Everyday moodiness, loss of jobs, overspending of money, even physical violence were things I had little or no experience with, and then suddenly too much. Ah, love.

Everything happens for a reason, right? I say bullshit. Drives me nuts when I tell my story and someone blurts out, "Well everything happens for a reason. Hee hee hee." There is usually a reason something happens, but that in no way is the same thing as something happening for a reason. Sometimes shit happens, let's face it. A typhoon hits a village: it's shit, it happened, and that is all there is to it. Let's not pretend thousands of innocent people were wiped out for a reason. My marrying an alcoholic was not some divine order teaching me how to take a bat in the back. It was my failure to get to know someone deeply enough. It was my failure to give myself enough credit that I did not need to marry someone quickly before they got away. There was a reason it happened; I admit I wanted to think someone beautiful loved me. But it did not happen for a reason.

So, how do you like me so far? Oh don't worry, I am not going to bog this story down too much with my whining about lost love and shit happening. I am just trying to provide some perspective, to share with you what this trip to the Great White North (it had been nothing but green so far by the way) meant to me, and where I was in terms of recovering from an unpleasant few years. I was not getting better because of this trip; I could not have done this trip had I not been getting better. If that makes any sense.

You are probably wondering what dreamboat of a car I am driving on this provincial journey. I bought a new car (a new old car, but you knew that) just for the trip, and I had to juggle the facts that I did not have a lot of money, that I could not afford something unreliable in a strange country, and the need for some degree of fuel economy. (The fact I was buying all my gas in litres is another story.) So all that spells: Corolla. Toyota. Old one of course, but so far I was pleased. I want to tell you I was getting good miles to the gallon, but as I mentioned I was buying litres, and moreover, driving kilometres. I have no idea, but we will go with yes, it was okay on gas. And yes, they do drive on the right hand side of the road in British Columbia. A buddy of mine from the golf club back home had been trying to tell me differently. He said he thought the rest of Canada drove on the right side, but it was on the left in BC because it is *British* Columbia. I thought he was joking, but upon reflection I don't think he was. Now I am trying to figure out what the border crossing would look like if suddenly the roads switched from right to left.

My biggest challenge was not the litres, but the speed limit signs. I got giddy when I saw the speed posted at 100 and hearkened back to one glorious trip on the Audubon in Germany a couple years earlier. Alas, 100 kilometres per hour is about 60 miles per hour. The other catch was the speed limit between Hope and Heaven changed about 62 times. 100. 90. 70. 90. 60. Small town ahead, 50. 40 even. That Canada's finest, the famous Mounties, did not pull me over was a miracle. Though that may be somewhat connected to the fact that Canada has more donut shops per capita than anywhere else in the world. No fooling, I am serious.

There it was, finally. The sign. Welcome to Heaven. Somehow, with a name like Heaven, you might expect a very ornate sign welcoming you. Not so in this Heaven. I am not implying there should be pearly gates or anything silly like that but I did imagine a big fancy sign, a mural perhaps, something with lots of fluffy white clouds contrasting against a deep blue sky. Instead, the sign was green with white lettering. Standard government issue. Population 4009.

There the sign stood, but there was nothing else in sight. Just farm fields. Soon I came to another sign that read, *Downtown Core 5 km.* I smiled as I tried to imagine a downtown core of a town that had a population of four thousand, and seemingly no buildings. I took the exit, and was pleased to see yet another sign, this one with a picture of a golfer and an arrow pointing left. I decided to forego the downtown core for now and head straight to my ultimate objective, the golf course. And yes, I was making the grand assumption there was just the one golf course in this little metropolis, but I could easily have been wrong.

What is known as "The Interior" of British Columbia is very mountainous, and Heaven lies in a massive, and extremely picturesque, valley. Thus the farm fields. Many of which, it turned out, were vineyards. Score. So as I describe the flatness of Heaven you have to also picture this flatness surrounded by massive mountains on a par with the Rockies. It felt like you were driving into Whoville. As I drove along a long, isolated, unpaved country road suddenly there it was...

John Westley

one single, large, white, palatial building. As I got closer it resembled less a palace and more something you might see in Gone With the Wind. It was the clubhouse of the Heaven Golf Club. Not Golf and Country Club, just Golf Club. It looked beautiful and not at all what I was expecting.

I turned into what was a very long driveway that fed up to the front of the club. In contrast to what I had seen to this point, it was a very busy place. Lots of Budget rental trucks, big white tents, communications trailers, vans, all the things you would expect to see at a professional golf event, but seemingly out of place here. A chill went through me. The notion and excitement of traveling and going into competition with a new golf swing I had confidence in was supplanted with a jolt of reality. The setting might have been surreal, but the competition was going to be real. The Canadian Tour is a developmental tour that feeds into the bigger tours that ultimately feed into the PGA Tour. This was no small town club championship, and that truth suddenly struck me.

Chapter ~~69~~ 4

I parked and walked around a bit, wandered through the clubhouse but basically tried to stay out of everybody's way. Everyone looked focused and busy, as was not surprising with a golf tournament just days away. I was surprised to get permission to hit golf balls on the driving range, though. A golf tournament can be a huge inconvenience to the members of a golf club so it is not unusual for them to cling to their range until the Monday of tournament week. But as there was no other range within one hundred kilometres theirs was made available for the early arrivals – people like me.

I have played in many tournaments before – all on mini-tours –so this really was nothing new. Yet somehow it did seem different. Whether it was because of the location, or my renewed confidence in my game I did not know. One of the true tests was about to come as I made my first swings on the range. I had played the best golf of my life in Tofino but the question remained whether my swing made the journey with me to Heaven, or was it back somewhere amongst the waves of Long Beach? I also had to acknowledge that the golf course in Tofino was not championship length, and I was playing with little or no pressure. Ah, how we golfers like to torture ourselves with questions and hypotheticals.

John Westley

The range was busy, and it was not hard to distinguish the pros from the members. I counted six members to six pros, not including myself. The pros looked good, but then they always do on a driving range. They all look like scratch handicaps when hitting alongside one another, and yet their scores can differ by a dozen shots in a single round, from six under to six over.

My answer – or at least an easing of my uncertainty – came quickly. Oh, I stretched, I made copious practice swings, I observed the others on the range, putting off my first shot. But that first shot eventually came, and it was a beauty. So was the next, and the next. Better yet, I did not let the continuation of my success get me too excited. I was relieved that my swing had made the journey but managed to settle down and just hit balls. Practice. Settle down, that was, until she came along.

I do not honestly think this had ever happened to me before – my heart skipped a beat. There is an old saying that, in terms of women, a seven on the street is a ten on the golf course. And we are not talking handicap. Well, this woman was a ten no matter where she was. And she was in Heaven. So was I.

As corny as it sounds, it was if she was walking toward me in slow motion. Your proverbial Clairol commercial with long blonde hair flowing, a modest but genuine smile on her face, a look to the left, and a look to the right, knowing she looked a million bucks yet somehow managing not to appear conceited. I was able to assess this so quickly because she was walking in slow motion, as I mentioned. Her shorts were not slutty, but definitely shorter than any golf club I knew of would allow. I do not know if I was more taken by her athletic legs or the fact she was carrying her clubs and not pulling them on a pink pull cart like all the women of Beaverton Golf Club back home. You could not miss the Muppet headcovers though. I think I was in love. What am I saying? I was in love. I wondered if she drank, though I did not say that out loud. I think I may have said, "*Holy crap*" out loud though. I'm not sure.

What I did say aloud, although I was careful to say it under my breath (albeit repeatedly) was, "*Please go to the stall next to me, please go to the stall next to me.*" Well guess what? She did not. No, she set up about six stalls down from me, between two good looking pros, both of whom seemed to know her and her them. I felt jealous. I did not even know who this woman was, and I felt jealous. I had no choice but to go back to my fabulous golf swing and try to put her out of my mind.

I did manage to focus and work through a routine with my clubs that I had started in Tofino. This routine finished with me hitting eight-irons to the 150 yard marker, until I hit the marker. That would be my permission to stop practicing and go home. Not that I had anywhere to stay yet. To my amazement I struck the marker on the second attempt. As it was made of metal, there was a big *clang* when the ball made contact after one hop. A couple of people looked up but I knew they knew anyone can hit a marker by accident. Not expecting to accomplish this wrap-up feat so quickly, I decided I ought to hit the marker a second time before giving myself the okay to quit. *Clang!* I did it again. This caused a few more heads to glance over. I admit I felt a bit chuffed.

Now my ego got to me, and I tried again. Miss. I tried once more. *Clang!* I stared down at the grass and the bucket of balls beneath me as I did not want anyone to catch me beaming like a little kid. As I pulled another ball toward me, I heard yet another *clang!* What? It was not me, I had not hit again yet. Someone else had hit my 150 yard marker. I had to look over and did so in time to see her at the top of her backswing. Perfect balance, weight slightly right of center, her long blonde hair now in a ponytail hanging as if she had not moved, she swung down. Swoosh... followed by *clang!* She glanced back with a cheeky little smile on her face. The nerve! I was instantly hard. Fine, you want to play games, game on. I swung... and missed. Hurriedly I set up another ball. *Clang!* It was her. I swung. *Clang!* Take that. She swung, and missed. Ha! I swung, *clang!* She was just about to hit another when she was interrupted by an announcement that came over the public address system,

"*Melissa Jones to the office please. Melissa Jones to the office.*" My gorgeous and unexpected competitor quickly threw her iron in her bag, slung the bag over her shoulder and made haste toward the clubhouse. This was fortuitous in many ways. First, I could now assume I knew her name. Second, as fun as our unspoken marker clanging competition was, where and how was it going to end? This way there was no clear victor, certainly no loser and best of all, because of the direction of the clubhouse, I got to check out her butt as she left. If she had had to walk toward me I cannot say what I would have done, save for the fact it probably would have been embarrassing. Probably? Who am I kidding? *Definitely* would have been embarrassing. I could see me stepping into my bucket of balls, or leaning on my golf bag and knocking it over; something. No, trust me, I speak the truth.

The bottom line was I had had a good day. The bottom line was that I had yet to secure a place to stay. I hit a few more balls, winding down with wedges, and then debated whether to practice some putting or not. As the evenings are wonderfully long in that part of the world in the summer, I decided to drive into the town of

Heaven (remember the downtown core?) to see if I could find a motel at half the rate of Vancouver prices. It did dawn on me that being summer, and with a golf tournament in town, rooms might not be going at bargain basement prices. It did not dawn on me – call me naïve – that there would be none going. The golf tournament had claimed every room in town that had not otherwise been booked by vacationers staying in this beautiful part of the world.

Before leaving the golf club I did learn that even though I was not an official entry into the tournament, because I was an official entry into the Monday qualifying tournament I was entitled to use of the locker rooms. This was huge. Not the locker rooms themselves, though they were big enough, but this meant if I were forced to stay in my car again (which it was looking like I would) at least I could shower, shave, and the other thing. I had not bathed since Tofino, and as the weather was quite warm a shower was seeming not just desirable, but downright necessary.

The other thing I learned, to counter the luxury of showering, was there was no way I was going to be able to park onsite overnight. Not that I expected to be able to, nor deep down would I want to be caught dead sleeping in my car at the golf club. Or, more accurately, caught sleeping.

What about the local campgrounds, you ask? Well, it seems Heaven is too good for camping. No camping allowed in the entire region of Heaven, B.C. Some thought it was a holdover from when the area was supposed to be Mormon Central, but that does not make a lot of sense. Others say they (the township) just wanted to avoid people buying lots and living like hippies in tents. Regardless of the reason, renting a space at a campsite was not an option.

I decided to try to somewhat recreate my accommodations of the night before. It was a longer drive, but I drove up the mountain and found a beautiful spot to park overlooking the majestic valley that was home to Heaven. I wondered if it might be cold at the higher elevation but it had been getting quite humid in the area, and where I parked it was just perfect. I was warm, dry, had a billion dollar view, all like the night before minus the fireworks, decadent mansions, and hot female jogger in the morning. Although, I did see a moose. Boy did I ever.

I have to paint this picture clearly. Imagine the setting as I have described it, me asleep in the passenger seat with it reclined as far as it would go, and the sun beginning to rise. Suddenly a small shaft of morning sunlight catches me in the eye and I awaken. I sit up, look to my right, only to be greeted by the enormous nose of a friggin' moose pressed up against the glass of my side window. Where Rocky was I had no idea, but there was Bullwinkle eying my leftover sandwich on the driver seat. He did not do anything, was aggressive in no way; he just looked at me, snorted and fogged up the window. By the time the window cleared he was trotting away.

I do not doubt for a second that he could have smashed the window with a slight butt of the head, but he had seemed merely inquisitive. He may well have been with the Neighborhood Watch, given the neighborhood I was in. Funny to think when a stranger in an old Corolla parks on a street of multi-million dollar homes no one bats an eye, but park in the middle of nowhere and the Moose Police are all over it. Ah, Canada.

Chapter ~~69~~ 5

It was now Sunday, one day until Monday qualifying. Given how accessible the golf club had been a day prior it was a no-brainer plan to return again to practice at length, but at the same time leisurely.

I regretted not asking if the dining room was available to us qualifiers. Qualifier-hopefuls, that is. I knew I could officially check in for the next day's round, and practice until the sun went down, but had neglected to ask about eating. All I knew, from what I could tell, was there was nothing that resembled a public restaurant for miles. Therefore it made sense to grab breakfast in town before heading to the golf course. And yes, I would also procure a sandwich to tide me over later in case I was stranded without food. If I *could* eat at the club, then all the better.

I found a truly Canadian diner this time, for my morning meal. Despite it being summer and warm out I chowed down on pancakes and back bacon as if my name was Jacques and I had spent the morning felling trees. I was quite excited about what was going on in my life at that point in time, and while I welcomed the opportunity to practice there was a part of me that wished I could just fast-forward to Monday morning.

I would be fibbing if I did not concede that my mind wandered to whether I might see Melissa Jones again that day. I wondered if she was a member or an employee of the club, or if she worked for the Canadian Tour? I somehow doubted she worked for the Tour as all their employees had been ant-busy setting up for the week ahead. That said, she did seem quite familiar with some of the pros on the range. And, *that said*, a woman that good looking makes friends quickly so the prior point may be irrelevant.

It was crazy of me to even fantasize about connecting with such a woman. And yet, we had already connected on a funny kind of level. I speak of our unspoken marksmanship competition. Clang-gate. That was both fun and exhilarating. Not to mention, it was also further validation of my new golf swing. I had been in a 'zone' that day; just focusing, swinging, hitting my target. Where normally the mere presence of a woman that beautiful would have made me crumble, I was encouraged by the fact I had risen to the occasion rather than collapsed.

I would have given anything to know what was running through her mind during our inadvertent and unusual encounter. Was it purely a lark for her, a chance to show off in front of the others? An opportunity, perhaps, to put me in my place? Or was she wondering who this gifted and mysterious golf pro was, striking the one-fifty marker with abandon? Wondering if *he* was the man who owned the 1999 Toyota Corolla in the parking lot? Her mind straying to the inevitable question of whether I wore boxers or briefs? I really hoped I would at least see her again.

The temperature was rising and the sun shining as I drove to the golf club, fully nourished. I would have opened the sun roof, if I'd had one. I pulled into the long Heaven Golf Club driveway and the presence of a tour event was that much more noticeable than it had been a day earlier. A procession of international and provincial flags lined either side of the unpaved driveway, big white trailers were visible to the right flanked by enormous, prototypical white tents to the left. At the end of this newly created corridor of ceremony stood the clubhouse. A Canadian Tour event, I was quickly learning, was a bit bigger deal than most of the mini-tour events I was used to.

I took my time, and practiced. And practiced. And practiced. But Melissa Jones was nowhere to be seen. I was delighted to learn that I was allowed to eat in the clubhouse, not just because it meant a meal beyond sandwiches (though ironically I did order a sandwich) but because it dawned on me she might work in the food and beverage department. If she did it was her day off, because I could not see her. It was Sunday after all. Not that Sunday is a quiet day at a golf club in the summer. Usually only senior staff get Sundays off. When I was an apprentice pro I liked working Sundays as it was the Head Professional's day off and despite being busy, the pro shop felt more relaxed. That was until he and his wife had their first baby. Then he started coming in on Sundays (as well as the other six days of the week) because he could get away with not working – something he could not get away with at home.

After lunch I went to the short game area and worked extensively on chipping and putting. I say "worked" but really mean practiced. I *worked* in Tofino so I could *practice* like this, on skills I had already learned. It is a great concept. Finally I moved to the sand trap and it was there that my heart skipped a beat. Second time in two days that happened. Now, this is the embarrassing part: no I did not see Melissa. Just her golf bag.

A powder blue Ping carry bag with those Muppet clubhead covers it was unmistakably hers. It stood next to the sand trap but she was nowhere in sight. I practiced at length (longer than I normally would, for obvious reasons) but I never did see her. I felt weird departing and just leaving her clubs sitting out there by the trap unattended. But I would have felt stranger had I dragged them into the pro shop saying, "I think someone left these out there." I might as well say, "Hi I'm the loser with a crush on some girl I just met – okay didn't really meet – yesterday, and I wasn't smelling her golf clubs honest, just checking the name tag and thought I should bring them in, in case it rained, even though there is no rain in the forecast for the entire week. Shall I put them over here?" I returned to my car and left Melissa's clubs right where they were, basking in the golden sun of twilight.

It was a gorgeous evening, so I decided to deposit my golf clubs into the trunk of my car and avail myself of the privilege of dining at the golf club. I had been quite thrifty during my Canadian journey to that point, and having stayed at the "Corolla Inn" the past two nights had managed to be a little under budget in terms of the allowance I had set for myself. Such is the life of playing mini-tours. While I had partaken of the cafeteria at lunchtime, this evening I was going to comb my hair and move up to experience the formal dining room.

I really was moving up as the dining room was on the second floor of what truly is one of the loveliest golf clubhouses I have ever seen. While I could have eaten on the patio, I had received enough sun that day and somehow it seemed more luxurious to sup inside the well appointed dining area, so that is what I did. The restaurant was not overly busy and I got a table by the window with a view of the golf course. Very flat, I could see all but three holes as they wound around a river that dissected the valley, mountains in the background guarding everything before them. I ordered the club sandwich.

While I felt spoiled with my unexpected access to the club, the range, and its facilities the one thing I had not been able to do was play the golf course before my qualifying round on Monday. That was a shame, but not at all surprising. Members have no access to their course the week of a tournament so the sanctity of their playing rights is strictly preserved the week prior. However, even members did not have access that day, Sunday. This was so that the grounds crew could do their finishing touches, mowing, pruning, digging bunkers and so on. And so the rules officials could finish marking the golf course with out-of-bounds and hazard lines and making sure the requisite stakes and markers were properly placed. Needless to say, it is a much greater challenge competing on a golf course you have never played before. If I did qualify, I would get a practice round in on Tuesday and another round on Wednesday playing in the obligatory pro-am. But for Monday qualifiers it was show up, tee up, and try not to throw up.

I knew that at least half the Monday qualifying field would be in the same boat I was, seeing and playing the golf course for the first time. The other half of the field is typically made up of locals who will have seen the course before, perhaps many times, but are generally not a threat. That group is nearly entirely made up of amateurs and can be divided into three sub-groups: low handicappers, people who think they are low handicappers, and people who plain old lie about their handicap just to get in. All three sub-groups pray they will play their career game, made up of career drives and career putts, not realizing that if the golf gods all aligned and they did qualify they would wet their pants on the first tee of round one and likely play their way into therapy. I would say they are harmless, but the last thing you want as a pro with true ambitions of qualifying is to be paired with one of the pant-wetters. A good pro can focus and block out external distractions… to a degree. But once the local dentist starts throwing his clubs and play slows to five-hour rounds, it can be a tough grind for even the best that have to bear witness. My point of all this is it was great to be able to sit and study the golf course with a bird's eye view.

I could see all the sand traps, the doglegs (holes that resemble a dog's leg, rather than being straight) and where the river crossed certain holes. I had a sense of the length of the course, the length of some holes versus others, and even how wide (or narrow) the fairways were. This little bit of insight would in theory be helpful on a practical level Monday but, just as importantly, on a psychological level it gave me the feeling I had a tiny leg up on my competition. My true competition, that was. Not Doctor Goodteeth.

I had just about exploited the crap out of my free and appreciated access to the Heaven Golf Club that day. Or had I? At that point it was clear the Corolla Inn would be my accommodation again, so it made good sense to go have a cleansing shower and shave. A hot tub came first though, only because it was there. Then shower, then shave (I have to do it in that order). I got back into my old clothes, however, as it did not make sense to sleep in a car in fresh clothes. In the morning I would take another shower and dress in my sporting best which I had managed to keep decent, hanging in a suit bag in the back seat. All in all it was a good day, and I had even started to let go of the pipe dream of bumping into one Melissa Jones.

Chapter ~~69~~ 6

Despite the mountains in the distance the sun still rose early Monday morning, sending sunshine through the windshield causing me to rise early also. It was funny to me how many times in the past I had to extricate myself from a nice warm bed to make a seven a.m. tee time, and here I was wide awake at five and did not tee off until eleven. I was seeing everything as opportunity, however, and this was an opportunity to stop for flapjacks, get to the club, check in, shower, dress, and warm up with time to spare.

Ow! As I got out of the car from the passenger side to go round to the driver's side I felt a small twinge in my back. Damn! Who would have thought that three nights sleeping in the passenger seat of a Toyota Corolla might have negative effects on one's back? Wasting no time yet moving cautiously, I moved away from the car and began to stretch, touching my toes. I had caught it in time, thank goodness. I stretched out the muscles in the problem area and did the same for the other side of my back as well. It is a fine line between tweaking your back, and having it go out on you. I was fortunate not to have had a long history of back ailments but I had had enough to know the difference; to know that I would be okay to play, but to be careful. My mind did not go to what I

John Westley

would do Monday night in terms of sleeping, but instead it remained purely focused on what I had to do to qualify that day. I was determined.

Having time on my side, I walked around a bit to make sure my back was properly stretched out before getting back in the car. Finally, I got in and drove to town for breakfast. As the morning went on my back felt better, not worse, so that was a very good sign. A real test would be when I made my first swings on the range, but first I had to check in to secure my position in the day's competition. You never really relax until you are checked in and know they have you in there, and are not in risk of forfeiting your spot. I also needed to get a caddy and was kicking myself that I had not done something about that the day before.

I located the registration tent – one of many that had been set up over the past few days.

"Dan Green. I believe I am at 10:57"

The gentleman, one of three officials sitting behind a folding table, perused a list of players on a clipboard.

"Red Green did you say?" the official asked with a straight face.

"Very funny," I replied. "You know, I did play with Red Green in a pro-am once."

"Serious?" he asked.

"Yes," I said. "He was a lot of fun, and not too bad a golfer. His claim to fame on the golf course was that he'd never lost a putt."

All three behind the table laughed in unison. It was a true story, too.

"Okay, Dan Green, 10:57, tenth tee so don't forget that. You are officially checked in. Anything else we can do for you sir?"

"Yes I need a caddy. Preferably someone who knows the course."

"Would someone breathing suffice? Not that there are any, the last caddy went a half hour ago," he explained.

"You're kidding."

"Would I kid you?" he asked.

"Yes, you kidded me two minutes ago, with the whole Red Green thing," I pointed out.

"You have a point," he said. "But I'm not kidding, I'm sorry, there are no caddies left at all."

I was instantly miffed at myself for not having done something about this the day before. No caddy? What was I going to do? I know it seems silly to non-golfers. I am a big enough man, I can carry my clubs. But it is a completely different experience when you can focus completely on what you are doing, and not where you are going to drop your clubs, or cleaning one after a shot. Not to mention, after tweaking my back, not having to carry would be a benefit.

Just as important is the camaraderie of a caddy. Someone to talk to, bounce ideas off of in terms of how to approach a shot, what club to use, many things - even if you are going to ignore their advice completely. I was crestfallen.

"I'm available."

The voice came from directly behind me. A female voice. I spun around, and there she was.

"Excuse me?" is all I could muster. Pathetic, I know.

"I'm available to caddy," Melissa replied, matter-of-factly.

"You?" I asked. I was not getting any less pathetic.

"Yes, me," she laughed. "Are you looking for a caddy or not?"

I swallowed before talking this time. "Well, I am, but it's just for Monday qualifying."

"I realize that, today being Monday and all. Where are your clubs?"

"They're right here," I said and pointed to air. "Er, I mean they're in my car. Ah, I can go get them."

"I'll come with you," she said nicely.

"NO!" I almost screamed. Well I did kind of scream it. "You stay here, I will go get them and meet you…"

"Here?" she asked? "Seeing as that is where you want me to wait?"

"Um, no, how about at the range?" I suggested.

"How about at the practice putting green?" Melissa countered.

"Sure, what's that?" I asked stupidly.

"It's the big piece of flat green grass with all the holes in it," she answered, with a smug smile. Who could blame her?

"Where's that? I meant *where's* the putting green? I know what a putting green is!" I said through the sweat that was dripping from my brow onto my big fat dumb lips.

"Good," she said, "because I was beginning to worry. Are you sure you don't want me to come help you get them from the car?" she asked sweetly. Everything about her was sweet.

"Yes, quite sure," I affirmed. Before walking away in the direction of the parking lot I made the mistake of looking toward the table of officials at the registration tent. And yes, they were laughing at me. Maybe not out loud in an obvious way, but they were laughing. I could feel it. At least I was not dumb enough to look back at her. Until she spoke again, that is.

"Excuse me, Mr. Green?"

I had no choice but to look back; she was calling me.

"Yes?"

"You're going to get your clubs from your car?"

"Yes," I confirmed. "I thought I said that?"

"You did," she agreed. Parking lot is that way," she said, pointing the other way.

"Oh," I said in a commanding whimper. And turned, and walked to the actual parking lot.

.

Chapter ~~69~~ 7

I was so screwed. Possibly the single greatest thing ever was happening to me and I was ballsing it up - *and* worried about how I was going to play that day with a goddess on the bag. I now had the distinct opportunity to make a fool of myself in front of her, while shooting a hundred. Way to go Dan.

What was I going to do? Call from the car and say I was sick? I could say my car was stolen. Damn my Oregon plates. I opened the trunk and pulled out my clubs. I changed into my golf shoes while trying desperately to think of what to do. I realized that there was nothing to do. Nothing but go out and face the music. Except in this case the music was the most incredibly sexy woman I had ever laid eyes on. But yes, I simply had to take a deep breath, suck it up princess, hand her my clubs without tripping or otherwise accidentally hurting her, head to the range, and pray that my teachings in Tofino were enough to overcome this unforeseen turn of events.

I was so screwed.

***

As corny as it sounds, it was as if extra sunlight was shining on her more than anyone else at the putting green as I arrived. She had

John Westley

white, soft-spike golf shoes on, short white athletic socks with a tiny bit of pink trim, and form fitting white shorts with a hint of pink at the pockets (again not extremely short but shorter than the dress code would allow at any golf club I had ever been to). Her legs were toned, tanned, and incredible. While not tucked in, her golf shirt – also pink - was extremely form fitting, hugging her incredible breasts and, with no buttons done up just more than a hint of cleavage was revealed. Her long blonde hair was tied back in a ponytail which poked through the back of a Ping golf cap – the cap being white but the letters on the front, pink. Never having been a detail-oriented man it was astounding to me that I had noticed all this in the matter of a few seconds. She extended her hand to me as I approached.

"I'm Melissa Jones," she said with a smile.

"Oh, hi," I started, "I'm Dan Green. Pleased to make your acquaintance." *Pleased to make your acquaintance?* Good god, I sounded like Eddie Haskell from Leave It to Beaver. At least I had managed to get more than two words out though, and without sounding like Porky Pig. "So, are you from around here?" Shit. Sorry, but seriously? It was out there now, so I awaited her answer.

"Yes, I am. Well not originally. I'm originally from Vancouver, but I have been living out here for fifteen years now."

Immediately I did some quick math in my head, but with only that to go on I really could not determine her age. I would need more clues. All I could trust was she was not less than fifteen. My gut guess was that she was about... thirty-two. I was never a believer that someone in their thirties could look twenty-five. They could look *amazing* for thirty-five, could even look better than most twenty-five year olds, but they could not look twenty-five. I wanted to say Melissa looked twenty-eight, twenty-nine, but there was a maturity and a confidence about her that belied that possibility. The more I thought about it, the more I put my money on thirty-two to win. Plus, I was thirty-five, so the math worked for me.

"Very beautiful. The area, I mean," I added, nervously. I was already worried that everything I said that day would be misconstrued or divulge my inner thoughts.

"What would you like to do first," she asked. Oh god, what would I like to do first? If she only knew! But I could not tell her that. No no no. My normal routine would be to visit the driving range first. As leery as I was of departing from my routine, today was already an unusual day and I thought I might relax quicker if I began with a putting warm-up.

"Why don't we putt?" I suggested.
"We?"

"Royal we," I explained. "I usually consider my caddy and me to be a team."

"I like that." She smiled.

"I never asked, have you caddied before?"

"Oh yes," she replied. "Many times, for my husband."

Instant disappointment. "Oh your husband played?"

"My ex-husband. And yes he played a bit, still does." My inner smile returned. And the feeling of nausea never left.

I began my putting routine which went very well, but for one thing. I was lag putting to one hole and Melissa was stooped down behind the hole, rolling the golf balls back to me. And yes, insert *she was touching my balls* joke here if you must, but that was not the issue. The way she crouched revealed the exquisiteness of her breasts all the more. To say that was a distraction – well, let's just say that Bill Murray setting off explosives all around me would have been less distracting. I think she may have even realized, as she backed away after a while. Perhaps she noticed the pool of drool accumulating around my feet. At least it was not landing on my nice clean golf shoes.

Suddenly it hit me. My nice clean golf shoes were the only thing clean about me -I was still in the clothes I had slept in! And practiced in the entire day before. Oh my god, how embarrassing. If there was a bigger doofus on the planet he was probably just about to board a space shuttle to planets beyond, leaving me alone on this one. I looked at my watch. I had time, if I wanted to go in to shower and change. Or change at least. But what was the point of just changing if I was still going to smell like my sandwich-infused car? And if I was going to hurriedly shower I ran the risk of slipping, banging my head, and knocking myself out. Hey, that was not such a bad option.

I took a deep breath and decided to stay the course. Wrinkled and all. She had accepted me thus far. Besides, I had to grow up; she was my caddy, we were not out on a date. I had a job to do that day, a single job, and that was to qualify for the week's event. Decision made, I calmed a little, and suggested we visit the range.

***

What was beautiful, though not as beautiful as Melissa, was that my session at the range went swimmingly. My work in Tofino had clearly moved from my head to my muscles and I could not have been more thrilled. The fact that I was under the pressure of qualifying, and the enormous pressure of having a caddy who was a ten both on and off the golf course, and was still striping the ball at ease was an enormous boon to me. My nervous excitement about Melissa countered my joyous excitement of swinging well, and I felt ready to tee it up.

"Shall we get a coffee?" I asked.

"Coffee?"

"Sure. You don't like coffee?"

"I love coffee," she replied. "But right before you play?"

"Sure, I always do. It calms me," I explained.

"Caffeine calms you?"

"Well maybe not the caffeine per se, but the warmth, and the routine," I said.

"Per se? A man who can talk," she said with a smile.

"I had a boss, a head pro, who constantly said *for say*. It drove me nuts but I never dared correct him." She laughed, I relaxed, we went and ordered two large coffees.

Chapter ~~69~~ 8

I will not bore you with a shot by shot account of my front nine (played on the back nine) except to say that I walked to the first tee (my tenth) at two under. Not one under a bench and one under a tree. Two under par. I was playing well. And Melissa was exemplary on the bag. We both went into compete mode and were, I thought, a formidable team. Part fantasy on my part, perhaps, but no one could argue it was not working. She was treating this as if we were in the fourth round of The Masters, not as if she was merely looping a meaningless round. I appreciated that. Needless to say, I was treating this as if it were the fourth round of a major as well. I was not being stupidly serious, and we did chat here and there, but I really did want to qualify and put my new found ability to the test in a tournament.

I managed two more birdies and one bogey on my second nine to finish the round with a 69. Even if this was not good enough to qualify I was pleased. I will not lie, I was also happy that I had acquitted myself well in front of Melissa. Even if I never saw her again, I knew I could walk away after an exciting and eventful day, with my head held high. In hindsight, if I had the whole day to do over again I would rather have shot 69 in wrinkled pants than 75 looking crisp and smart.

John Westley

So the question became: was 69 good enough to qualify? One of the benefits of teeing off late was I did not have to wait long to find out. There was a 66 ahead of me, and another 69, and that was all that mattered. I qualified. Thank you. The top three, of which I was one, secured spots in the field for Thursday. I could not have been happier. Though I actually was – happier, that is – moments after the announcement as Melissa spontaneously threw me a big hug. To be clear, *any* caddy, male or female, might hug their player with the good news of qualifying, but needless to say this hug sent feelings that permeated throughout my loins. After a shocked delay that was probably not as long as it seemed, I hugged back and we remained embraced for a moment. That embrace also was probably not as long as it seemed, and as much as I could have stayed locked there until my tee time on Thursday it was me who pulled away - purely out of a feeling of self-consciousness.

"Congratulations," Melissa said.

"Thank you," I replied, adding, "Shall we get something to eat?"

"To eat?" she asked.

"Oh, I'm sorry, I didn't mean to imply you didn't have plans, I just thought you might be hungry," I explained. Perhaps my best put together sentence of the day to that point.

"No, I am hungry. Let's eat," she said with a purr, although I think the purr was just wishful thinking on my part.

"Dining room?"

"Hmmm," she replied. Do you mind if we eat in the caf?"

"Not at all, food is food. Do you mind if I go have a quick shower before we eat?" I asked.

"Of course. I will do the same." The mere thought of her showering sent chills. The good kind.

"Can you?"

"Can I what? Shower?" she asked, with a confused look on her face.

"I mean, are you allowed –"

She interrupted: "Oh, yes, I'm a member here. Sorry, I never mentioned that."

"So meet you in the cafeteria in… 30 minutes? That enough time?"

"Perfect," she said, and smiled. I turned to grab my clubs when I felt another twinge in my back. It must have been noticeable as she reached out and steadied me. "Are you okay?"

"Oh yes, it's just minor, from sleeping in my car." What an idiot. What a big mouth.

"Sleeping in your car? Why have you been sleeping in your car?"

I bent down to touch my toes and straighten out my back. "There was no room at the Inn, so to speak. I never imagined I wouldn't get a room anywhere, and camping seems to be sacrilegious here, so I had no choice."

"Well you're not sleeping in your car again. You have a tournament to play; you can't run the risk of making your back worse."

"Well I don't exactly have a choice," I explained.

"Yes you do," she responded.

"I do?" I asked with a laugh. "And what's that?"

She looked at me seriously. "You'll stay with me."

Chapter ~~69~~ 9

"With you?" I asked, my astonishment obvious. "Stay?" I asked again. "With you?"

"Of course, "Melissa replied. I have a huge five-bedroom house, you have a bad back, you've got a tournament to win, and you're sleeping in your Corolla."

I had about a dozen things I wanted to say and yet the first thing that blurted out was, "How did you know I had a Corolla?"

The look on Melissa's face suddenly changed. "I'm sorry, I shouldn't be assuming you want me to caddy for you all week. If you don't want me – "

"Oh I want you!" Okay, *that* came out wrong. "Of course I want you to caddy for me," I clarified.

"Even if you didn't want me to caddy, I still have plenty of room.

"No, that's not it at all," I said.

"Well, what *is* it?" Melissa asked.

"There's no *it*," I replied, fumbling. "I just don't want to impose."

Melissa laughed an intoxicating laugh before saying, "It's not an imposition; we're friendly people here, you're in Heaven."

Yes I am I thought to myself.

"It just makes sense is all. I won't make much money if you don't do well, and you won't do well if you aggravate that bad back of yours sleeping in your car." Okay, that was the second time she used the term 'bad back'. That made me feel old.

"It's a little bit tight," I conceded, "no doubt from sleeping in the car, but I don't actually have a *'bad back'* per se.

"Per se," she added, mimicking me. "But you don't actually have somewhere to stay."

"No, no I don't."

"Then that settles it, you're staying with me. Unless... that makes you feel uncomfortable." I'm sure it was just a coincidence that she took off her golf cap at that moment, and her astonishing blonde hair fell to her shoulders. Make me feel uncomfortable? How could I possibly describe to her the level of discomfort I was experiencing?

"Why should I feel uncomfortable?" I asked, an attempt to defy my true feelings. "If you're sure you don't mind."

"I don't. So deal then."

I managed a smile. "Deal." Of course, for all I knew, it was a dumb-ass grin. "So, meet you in the cafeteria in thirty minutes?"

"No!" she said in an incredulous tone.

"No?"

"If you're staying with me it makes more sense to eat at my place."

"I should still shower," I mentioned.

This will come as a shock to you," she said, flashing her irresistible smile, "but my house has a shower."

***

Melissa's 'house' was almost as palatial as the golf course's clubhouse. When someone says 'five bedrooms' you know this is not going to be a small house, but I had grown up in a fairly pedestrian four-bedroom. Melissa's five-bedroom only had one more bedroom, but the smallest among them was as big as my parents' master. The true divider is in bathrooms and garages. Her home had three more bathrooms and two more garages. Not to say you could not park a Smart Car in one of the larger bathrooms, but that is moot.

I parked my Corolla in Melissa's driveway, half expecting her to ask me to park it a block or two away. One thing I was learning about her, though, was that while she looked – and probably had – a million bucks, she in no way came off as superficial. She sure would not be inviting some fledgling Oregonian tour pro with an old Corolla to stay if she was.

The front entrance was enormous. I have often thought that a key thing separating the rich from the poor, other than the obvious dollar signs, is tidiness. You do not see many messy rich homes. But then, they have so much damned space to put stuff. I have three tour bags and two other sets of clubs just sitting out in my living room at home. She probably had a storage shed the size of my living room somewhere on this plantation.

Melissa invited me to drop my things in 'my room' and then gave me the cook's tour. I will skip all the predictable oohs and ahs stuff and get to the shocker. In fact, she was not even going to show me the shocker. She showed me the mud room but was going to skip the shocker room all together.

"Is that the help's quarters?" I asked with a whimsical smile.

"Oh, that's just my ex's study, he hasn't cleaned it out yet. Just a bunch of old golf stuff, but I guess you might get a kick out of some of it," she said as she opened the door. She let me go in first, and my jaw dropped as I did.

Her ex-husband's 'study' was a shrine to golf. Not just a shrine to golf, but a shrine to everything *he* had won in golf. Melissa Jones' ex-husband was former world number one golfer Andy Jones! Winner of a dozen titles on tour, including two separate majors, and still in the Top 40 on the money list. When she said she had caddied for her ex-husband I never in a million years connected her name Jones to Andy Jones! Her name was Jones, after all. What a dwarf I felt suddenly, not that I was feeling a giant before.

"Wait a minute," I said.

"Seen enough?" she said.

"No no no no. You've been holding out on me."

"Oh, hardly," she scoffed. "I barely know you. I carried your clubs for eighteen holes. I was supposed to divulge my life story to you?"

"Hmm," I said. She kind of had me.

"Hell, you were trying to hide your Corolla from me." That prompted a laugh out of me, and she joined in. Until it got awkward. There had been no shortage of awkward that day. "You roam around in here if you must. I'm going to go shower, then start dinner. You can shower when I shower, if you like."

"Excuse me?" My jaw would have dropped had it not already been resting on the floor of Andy Jones' study.

"There's a shower in your room," she added. I was still in a daze. "An ensuite?"

"Wha? Oh! Yes, of course. Yes, okay I will mull around here for five and then grab a shower. In the ensuite." Melissa smiled, turned, and left me to wander through the Heaven International Golf Museum. There were several trophies from all ranks of golf, but it was the photographs I got the biggest kick out of. Photos of trophy presentations, of hobnobbing with celebrities. There was one photo of Andy with Bob Hope, taken presumably before Hope died but I could not be certain. There was another of

Andy with Tiger Woods, Wayne Gretzky, and Michael Jordan. That almost impressed me more than the two major wins.

I had obviously lost track of time when Melissa gently knocked on the study door. I turned to see her leaning in the doorway, drying her hair with a towel. She was in silky running shorts and a very tight tank top. Her hair had been pulled to one side as she stroked it with a towel. "You haven't showered yet?" She was right.

"Oh shoot, I lost track of time. I'll go right now."

"And I'll get dinner started," she said, without moving. I walked to the study door fully expecting she would leave or move, but she did not. She remained there, half in the doorway, drying her hair. Continuing with the theme of 'awkward' I paused at the doorway a moment, and then did my best to slip by her without seemingly intentionally brushing up against her breasts. Even with my sincerely best efforts there was still a hint of contact (which sent a jolt of excitement through my body by the way) as I passed by and made my way to my room, and a very cold shower.

***

By the time I had dressed and arrived in the kitchen the delicious aroma of meat and sauce filled the room. Melissa was at the stove, her back to me. She had changed clothes of course, now wearing an extremely flattering, and very tight to form, floral summer dress. Small straps clung to her tanned shoulders and the back was cut very low, leaving me – for the moment – wondering how low cut the front of her dress might be. Her blonde hair was down (and now dry). I took the opportunity to peruse her toned and well defined body from the top down – pausing for some time at her ass, noting how one cheek would flex as she would take a side step in one direction, and the other cheek would flex as she stepped in the other direction. After my eyes continued down, past her shapely calves, I finally arrived at her feet which were bare, and very white where her tan had obviously stopped in favour of short little sport socks. This was almost surprising for someone who, while not overtly superficial, clearly cared about how she looked and you would think wore an abundance of sandals and summer shoes this time of year. In fact, the contrast between her white feet and richly brown legs gave the illusion she was indeed wearing white sport socks, though she was not.

It defies logic but this small evidence of golfer's tan cast my mind back to my junior days. In the summers the only people who played more golf than the kids was the old geezers. They played every single day, all of them to a man dressed in golf shirts, long golf shorts, and equally long knee socks as had been the custom in their day. You would see these old guys in the showers after a round, their old bony legs pasty white but for an incredibly rich, uniform brown band of tan about three inches in height that wrapped around their knees where socks and shorts had failed to meet. It was a hilarious sight. Melissa turned to face me and instantly all thoughts of old men in showers magically disappeared.

"Oh, hello. How long have you been standing there?" she asked.

"I just got here," I lied.

"I'm whipping up some burgers, I hope that's okay."

"You look amazing," I inadvertently said, not lying but regretting I had lost control of my mouth.

"Pardon me?"

"I said that sounds amazing, I love burgers."

"Not too boring? They are gourmet burgers."

"Not at all – hey I would have settled for McDonald's."

"Oh please! After you eat these you will never want to eat fast food ever again."

"That could ruin me for life, then," I said with a laugh.

***

We sat out on Melissa's deck overlooking… nothing. Absolute, yet beautiful, nothingness. Her house was on the perimeter of a subdivision, bordering on a sanctuary of some sort which meant, in theory, no houses would be built there in the future (until some politician got paid off, at least). So our view was open fields, bathed in that golden evening sun that photographers refer to as 'magic hour'. Mountains in the distance enveloped the entire scene.

We talked about golf, naturally, but not ad nauseum. Some of that talk extended to places we had journeyed, and while she had traveled in a completely different style than I had, we had hit a number of the same places. However, our conversation eventually turned to her marriage to Andy Jones.

I had been on many a date (not that this in any way counted as a date, despite any wishful thinking that may have existed on my part) where the conversation inevitably turned to my date castigating her ex-husband, her ex-boyfriend, hell even her x-box. It could go on for hours and was never entertaining. Yet here *I* was initiating the telling of the tale of her break-up with one of the world's best golfers.

"In the end," she said, "it was about sex. He wanted sex every day, and I couldn't live with his having it every day, especially when I was not there."

"I can understand that," I said empathetically.

"It's always about sex or money," she stated.

"Or alcohol," I added, and then went on to tell her my tale, after which she commented,

"I feel your pain, and don't disagree with what you have said but in the end one could argue it still came down to sex. When the sex was great, you were happy even when she was drinking, and when the sex disappeared so did your happiness."

"Yes," I concurred, "but the sex was just a symptom of how I thought she felt about me. When the sex was great, I thought she loved me, and when the sex disappeared, I thought she hated me. Which it really did seem."

"Really she hated herself," Melissa added.

"Yes, I suppose so, though I have never really understood that concept. Especially amongst narcissists."

"Now," Melissa started, while coyly picking up some dishes to take them inside, "this begs the question, what do you consider to be great sex?" What a question to ask while at the same time leaving the table! What a question to ask as I caught myself checking out her ass and wondering what it looked like naked? What was I to do? There was clearly no one nearby to overhear us, but was I to yell my response, or get up and follow her in like a puppy dog? In heat, no less. And this was not about the weather. As dense as I had been several times the past few days, the right answer came to me. I picked up some of the other dirty dishes and brought them, too, into the kitchen.

"I'm sorry, I didn't hear the question," I fibbed as I placed the dishes I was carrying on the counter near the dishwasher.

"Yes you did," she said, not skipping a beat. "Everyone talks about great sex, but what does that really mean? Is it where love is involved, or does doing it on furniture suffice?" she inquired, quite frankly.

"Doesn't that depend on who is involved?" I asked.

"I guess it does," she said. "Let's say you then."

"You then," I said and laughed.

"C'mon! What for you defines great sex? You have one minute to think about it while you bring those chairs inside for me, please." She pointed to the chairs we had been sitting on, which came from the dining set inside. 'Much more comfortable' she had explained earlier. I went back out to consider not just what my answer to her question was, but what I would say out loud (two completely different things, akin to which movie you think will win Best Picture, and which you thought actually was the

best picture) while I retrieved the dining chairs.
Perhaps – obviously – distracted by the subject
matter I failed to open the sliding glass door
fully, forcing me to twist to get the chairs
through. That was a bit of a mistake. I twisted,
and then I felt the spasm. Same place as before,
perhaps a little more intense. And, I was stuck,
which meant I could not stretch out the spasm
and I could feel it pulling tighter.

"Um, excuse me," I called out to Melissa,
not very loudly. I do not think she heard me but
luckily she was on her way back from the
kitchen anyway. She saw me. Laughing, she
said,

"Are you stuck?"

"Um, ya," I said. The look on her face
turned to one of concern as she reached for one
of the chairs and asked,

"Are you in pain?"

"Um, ya," I confessed.

"Oh my god," she exclaimed, taking one
of the chairs from me. "Drop the other chair,"
she instructed.

"It's too nice," I said.

"It's *a chair!*" I dropped the chair. Melissa
reached for and took my arm. She assisted me as
I side-shuffled through the doorway, and sat me
down on the chair that had been taken from me
a moment earlier. "Where?" she asked.

"Where what?" I asked dumbly.

"Where is the pain? Where in your back?"

"Oh it's okay," I said.

"*Where?*" she demanded.

"Lower right," I replied quickly, reacting to her insistence. Her deceptively powerful hands moved to the area of my back that was relentlessly contracting and she began to knead the muscle. I cannot say if I was more thrilled at the instant relief from the pain, or the fact this beautiful woman had her hands on me. The former was a welcomed relief, the latter was, was, well it was more than sensual. She pulled up my shirt and continued to work her magic, and as she did my brain went crazy. Her hands were soft but her grip on my muscles so strong.

The combination of touch and caring in one breath sent feelings through me I had never experienced before. My mind shot back to a time in my marriage when, after playing thirty-six holes on a very hilly Hawaiian golf course, I got cramp not in one leg, but both. Being unable to stand I lay myself down on the floor, and while I tried to tend to one leg the other would cramp more severely. I would turn my focus to that leg, only to then have the first one tighten even more. The pain was excruciating and no one, me included, could have avoided screaming from it. This annoyed my then-wife, who was trying to catch up on Grey's Anatomy. Finally, upon realizing (or so I thought) that I was in sincere agony she stood up from the couch but rather than help, walked around me and got a beer from the bar fridge. She returned, towered over me, and asked what was happening. I explained I was having severe cramp in both legs and, satisfied with my answer, she returned to the couch at the precise time the commercial break ended. This was the kind of love I was used to. So for a virtual stranger to be taking such immediate and caring action affected me beyond the very real fantasy of feeling her hands on my skin. Not by a whole ton, mind you, but it made the entire experience somewhat surreal.

"Is that any better?" Melissa asked.

"Oh it is, it is, thank you. You're a miracle worker."

"We need to get you on the table," she said.

"Excuse me?" was my automatic response.

"On the massage table. I have one downstairs; do you think you can manage a flight of stairs?"

"I'm not 80," I replied mockingly.

"C'mon then," she said flipping her head (and thus her golden locks) toward the stairway to the basement, which had not been a part of the cook's tour earlier. I responded obediently, not thinking resistance was an option and besides, despite the pain in my lower back this evening was just getting more and more interesting.

I could have managed the stairs easily, but allowed Melissa to put one arm around my waist and help me. The stairs led to any man's dream basement. There was a full sized billiard table to the left (when a billiard table is to the left as opposed to filling the entire room, you know it is a big room), a massive flat screen television mounted on the wall to the right, and at the end of the room a glass door led to the most sophisticated wine cellar I had ever seen. Just to the right of the wine cellar was another door, a conventional door, that led to what clearly was the "massage room". A massage table filled the center of the room, piles of perfectly folded white towels lined the shelves beyond, and there were two what I like to call 'comfy' chairs in one corner.

"Take off your shirt," she directed.

"What?" I replied. "This seemed to be my default response to anything she said that might provoke fantastic thoughts in my little brain.

Without skipping a beat she explained, "Take off your shirt and lie down."

"On the table?" I asked. I truly am smarter than I sounded, I promise, but one could be forgiven for not believing me.

"No, on the floor. Of course the table, silly. Lie down on your tummy; your face goes where the hole in the table is."

"I figured that," I said, in a useless attempt to not sound as stupid as, well, I had sounded up until then. I took off my shirt, looked around, and threw it on one of the comfy chairs. Melissa promptly picked it up off the chair and hung it on a hook on the wall nearby. I lay down on the table, and yes, my face was at the correct end. That said, once she put her soft, strong hands on me again I realized a similar opening in the table would have come in handy, further down. If you know what I mean. I cannot pretend I was completely comfortable.

Despite my 'injury' being lower down my back, she began by massaging my shoulders. "Relax," she said. Ya, right. One hand on each shoulder at first, then double-teaming the left shoulder, then the other. The intensity was light at first, but got progressively stronger, firmer. Not a word was spoken. That was a shame, as it might have made it easier to hide my moans, despite them being directed to the floor. Melissa then moved down my back, repeating the scenario of starting softly, then getting firmer.

I was torn. The light touch that was introduced to an area of my back was scintillating, but as the massage got firmer Melissa would lean in more, to apply strength, and invariably I would feel the touch of her breasts against my bare skin. I reached levels of hard I did not know existed, and while I was extremely grateful she could not see that part of my anatomy it became increasingly difficult to lie flat, on my stomach. Heaven forbid she should ask me to roll onto my back; I might knock the overhead light fixture off.

It took some time – time I did not begrudge in the least – for her to get to the problem area, my right lower back. I then realized the method to her madness – that area was sore from not just the initial pull, but also the massaging she had given it upstairs. But not as sore as it was twenty minutes prior, when my 'Massage in Heaven" commenced. Now she went to work. With seemingly tireless strength in her hands she dug in deep to the muscle, massaging, rubbing, and kneading. It was the strangest combination of excruciating pain and joyous sensation. While I could have almost fallen asleep at earlier points in the massage, there would be no concept of drifting off while she worked on the pulled portion of my back. Still, it was as if being awoken from a stupor when she finally spoke.

"Undo your belt please." Do I even have to mention what I said in response?

"What?"

"You need to loosen your belt, so I can get to the muscle immediately below the pull."

"Seriously?"

"You're an adult, I'm an adult, if you want me to fix this I need you to undo your belt. Trust me." Trust *her?* It was not *her* I was worried about! She could take all the liberties with me she wanted; I was just worried about her noticing how excited I was to be near her, to smell her, to feel her hands on me. And now she was going to go below the belt? In a good way? I reached down, somewhat awkwardly, and undid my belt.

She did as she had said she would; her hands began to massage the muscle immediately below the area she had been working on hither. It appeared my unbuckling was not enough, as Melissa seemed to get frustrated with my pants getting in the way. So she methodically pulled my pants down, just a bit, revealing only my undie-covered buttocks. This prompted me to close my eyes and send a little, silent *thank you* to my dear departed mother, who had always insisted despite anything else, that I wear clean and new underwear. Now I knew why, and I was more grateful than I could ever explain.

Melissa was nothing if not balanced. As she had done to this point, whatever area she worked on one side of my body was matched on the other. The only question was, *how low would she go?* I thought I was joking when I asked that question to myself, only to almost jolt right off the massage table when she began to massage my buttocks. First the left cheek, then the right. Balanced. Oh my god, what would she do next? What would I do next? So far I had just done a whole lot of nothing, soaking in one of the most exhilarating experiences of my life. Did I say *one of*? If she did go further, into uncharted territory, what would I do? What should I do? What would she expect or want me to do? My brain was going crazy... my tiny little brain in my big fat head that was now slotted face down into the hole of a folding table.

Slap!

Melissa gave my butt a good whack, and said, "Feel better? I think that's about all my hands can handle today." I replied, but of course you have to picture my response being mumbled down to the floor below me,

"Much better. So much better. Incredible in fact. Thank you so much."

"You better stand up," she said, "and see how your back responds." I did as she suggested and truthfully I felt great. Beyond the obvious reasons. I stretched, I bent over, I touched my toes. No pain. Incredible. *She* was incredible.

"I'll let you pull up your pants and then you can come meet me upstairs for a drink before bed." Good god what a moron I was. Complete and absolute freakin' moron! There I was stretching and touching my toes *with my pants down around my ankles!* Quickly I hiked them up – I swear both feet left the ground momentarily as I did – and fastened my belt around my waist. As Melissa left the 'massage room' I reached for my shirt that was hanging, much as I ought to have been.

John Westley

Chapter ~~69~~ 10

I went upstairs and already there was a drink poured for me. At least I assumed it was for me as there were two drinks poured, and one hot babe and one dumb ape in the house. The drinks were on the coffee table by the couch, in the small lounge right off the kitchen. I picked up one of the drinks, but then had a decision to make: where to sit? I had three choices… couch, lounge chair, or lounge chair. Now, if I chose the couch it might look a little presumptuous that I was expecting or hoping for Melissa to sit on the couch too. However, if I sat on one of the lounge chairs I was a) ruling out all hope of us sitting together and b) possibly sending a message that I wanted to sit on my own. Clearly over-thinking, as I was wont to do and not wanting to send the wrong message I decided to run the risk and sat myself down on the couch. It was a big couch, so if I sat to one end there was plenty of room for her to sit down if she wanted to, without feeling like she would be sitting on my knee. That said I knew if I *did* sit on the couch, and *she* chose one of the comfy chairs, I would have to suck it up buttercup and not be too heartbroken.

I was almost nodding off when Melissa returned to the room. Picture, if you will, my first image as her tanned and proportionately muscled quads passed by me at eye level. I sat up from my slouch as she sat down – on the couch – and reached forward to pick up her drink. No longer in her sundress, she was now wearing athletic shorts again and a white, baggy, v-neck t-shirt. I had no idea she did baggy. But it worked. Hell, everything she wore worked. I am quite sure she could wear a garbage bag to a Halloween party and win best costume.

"You changed?"

"I had to," she replied. "You didn't notice?"

"Notice what?"

"I ripped my dress."

"When?"

"Giving you your massage. The front split." Oh good god. And I missed it? I was so busy doing calisthenics with my pants down around my ankles I did not even notice this well endowed beauty had split her dress, at the front no less.

"I feel terrible, that's all my fault. Can I please replace it for you?"

"Oh no, don't be silly. I have plenty of sundresses, and it's an easy fix."

"Then let me fix it for you." For once it was her turn to say,

"What?"

"Let me fix it for you; I can sew."

"You can?" she asked, clearly quite surprised.

"Sure, my mom taught me. Forced me to

John Westley

learn, more like it. She got tired of fixing my socks or buying me new ones, so it started with that. Then, because I grew like a weed, my pants kept having to be let down so she taught me how to do that. After a while you could tell how old I was by counting the rings at the bottom of my pant legs." Melissa burst out laughing, almost spitting her drink.

"Well I might let you fix it, not because you need to but because *I* need to see you do it!" Melissa said with an alluring smile.

"You'd be surprised how many pros on tour can sew."

"The only thing my ex could sew was wild oats. I certainly never saw any of the other pros sewing, or doing needlework of any kind," she laughed.

"Well that's the big tour. Us guys on the mini tours don't get free clothes given to us at every stop. And we can't take anything in to be fixed because if we're in Maine the thing won't be ready 'til we're in Toledo. You kind of have no choice."

"You know other pros that can sew?" she asked incredulously.

"Sure, at least a dozen. Mind you I taught a few of them. It's not like we don't have the time."

"So what else can you do? Your own laundry?"

"Don't insult me," I said as I turned my

80

head away from her, melodramatically.

"Iron?"

"*All* golf pros iron, c'mon."

"Not when there's a drycleaner nearby."

"Big tour. We're talking mini tours here. Pros using a dollar store calculator to see if they can afford gas to get to the next event do *not* take their *slacks* to the drycleaners!" Melissa laughed again. A big hearty laugh, and then pulled her legs up onto the couch as she crossed them and turned to face me, now holding her drink cozily with both hands. She was on the far end of the couch but I was thrilled that the couch had been her choice at all.

"I haven't laughed like this in a long while," she declared.

"You're kidding," I said, quite seriously. "You seem such a happy type."

"Oh I stay positive, and I get no extra energy from walking around with a frown on my face. And I genuinely enjoy people but it has been a long time since I laughed. A sincere laugh, I mean. Not just to be polite." This was a side of Melissa I had not seen coming. I was so caught up in my own infatuation with her, I had not considered that she was – or felt – anything less than perfect.

"That's a shame; I never would have guessed that. And you have such a great laugh. I noticed it immediately on the range Saturday," I admitted.

"Oh, you saw me on the range?" she asked. That one threw me for a loop. Of course I saw her on the range. I took a sip of my drink but there was none to sip. "Your glass is empty, let me fix that," she offered. She leaned forward from her position on the couch, causing her t-shirt to droop down at the front. As she took my empty glass I could not help but see her perfect, almost muscular, and seemingly real breasts mere inches before me. Thank god the glass was empty, because I would undoubtedly have spilled whatever was in it with this incredible distraction. She got up and turned, allowing me to see the backs of her legs as she waltzed away, unaware that her shorts on one side had got tucked up, revealing her right butt cheek in all its splendor. I had only had one drink, but a teetotaler would have felt as inebriated as I was with all the sensory input I had been treated to that magical day.

Melissa returned with my drink – a rum and coke by the way, and how she knew I will never know – and sat back down on the couch. Same spot. I was hoping it would have been closer but I – chicken shit that I am – would probably have done the same thing. Not that I could in any way call Melissa a chicken shit. Taking a strange American into her home, making him dinner, healing his back – crazy maybe, but not chicken shit.

I do not know if I can define the next ten minutes as awkward, or not. They certainly were silent. Silence can be awkward, or it can be a sign of compatibility, or of unspoken comfort. I did feel comfortable. So comfortable I fell asleep – not for long though, as the sound of my own snore woke me. I am not a snorer as a rule, but am good for one good blast as I fall asleep, which often then wakes me. Kind of like an internal alarm. A catch-22 as it were. I looked over at Melissa and she was asleep; fast asleep. You hear people talk about how lovely and innocent a child looks when they are asleep, well the same could be said of Melissa. I debated picking her up and carrying her to her room. Requisite to the debate was this could be interpreted on one side of the ledger as chivalrous and romantic, and equally valid on the other side, as creepy. The internal debate ended quickly as, chivalry and creepiness aside, it would have been just plain dumb given the state of my back. I could see it now: *Golf Pro Drops Half-Dressed Caddy On Stairs, Film At Eleven.*

I glanced around and spotted a nice big yet thin blanket on a chest near the fireplace. The room was not cold but somehow draping the blanket over her gorgeous body seemed both fitting and apropos. With a soupcon of chivalry thrown in, one could argue. I know I would. It was so very tempting to lean down and give her a gentle kiss on her forehead; a thank you for all she had done for me not just that day, but was offering to do for me that week. I leaned down, and down, my lips mere inches from her forehead. But that was as near as I would go, deciding instead to take the dirty glasses to the kitchen and retire to my room. The day had been perfect; there was no need to tempt fate with a silly little kiss. Don't you agree?

Chapter ~~69~~ 11

Tuesday morning arrived just as any morning did. In Heaven. When you have just met the most heart encapsulating woman you have ever laid eyes on. And get to take her to breakfast. She swayed me away from my beloved flapjacks and toward an eggs benny that was more dessert than breakfast. Eggs Benedict was one of those things – like salmon, and white wine – that I never craved and yet always marveled at how enjoyable they were when I did have them. Yet, for some strange reason, that never led to future cravings. Though on this day, practice round Tuesday, I would have been inclined to suggest that from then on Eggs Benedict would hold a dear and special place in my heart.

It was back to business once we reached the golf course. It really needed to be. It was important for me to remember that I was in Heaven for a reason. That there was perhaps an even higher purpose developing did not escape my daydreamy little mind, but I was playing well and needed to explore where that might take me. I was more than playing well; a metamorphosis was occurring within my game. My life too, clearly, but I was trying not to think about that – not while at the golf course at least.

Some people have life-altering occurrences... that change them internally. For some it may be having a child, a change in vocation, a near-death experience. For me, it was as if something happened to me the moment I got onto the ferry from Seattle to Victoria, enroute to the surf capital of Canada, Tofino. I felt lighter, I felt positive, I felt open. Open to change and open to possibilities. I also opened myself up to listening to logic, rather than convention, in terms of the golf swing. Every day was a good day, and each day better than the one before. One might consider having to sleep in your car a low point, but in my case it had me on top of the world. Hurt your back, that must be a bad thing. For me it led to one of the nicest evenings of my life. Here I found myself readying for a Tuesday practice round, old hat for a journeyman tour pro, yet I felt born again. The best part was that I could picture *not* playing well, and not caring. That would be something new for me. At that point unverified, but it was how I felt.

As for Melissa, it was not clear whether I felt wonderful because of her presence, or if she was present because of my transformation. I had to remind myself that while her caddying for me – let alone her inviting me to stay at her house for the week – was a gift from heaven, in Heaven, nothing was actually going on here. At times I felt like a high school kid with a new girlfriend, only to come crashing back down to earth with the realization that she had simply offered to caddy for me. C'est tout. And, because she is a nice person, she invited me to stay upon discovering I had been sleeping in my car. Nothing to see here, please disperse. There was nothing going on. There was *nothing* going on.

I so wanted there to be something going on.

Of course, a practice round was going on. And it was going extremely well. Now, in all honesty, while you want your practice round to go well it can often mean nothing. I had had plenty of good practice rounds that led to missed cuts, and terrible practice rounds that led to weekends where I was in the hunt. What was different this time around was my mindset. I was getting used to playing well. I was not just playing well, I was playing with confidence. It is a dime a dozen the guy who plays well, with *no* confidence he will play the same way tomorrow. I simply felt like this was the new me. As lacking in confidence as I may have seemed in front of Melissa off the golf course, it was a completely different story on the golf course. Again, I did not know if she was the cause of it or the beneficiary, but I did not care. I was having fun and my heart felt full, as corny as that may sound.

***

A practice round is rarely a proper round of golf. It is what more amateurs should do, in the summer, after dinner, when the golf courses are inexplicably quiet and two or more balls may be played. You can try drives from different tee boxes, drop a ball in a fairway bunker, and putt from and to various points on the green where you think (or know) the pins will be. Melissa was extremely helpful, especially on the greens, as she knew the golf course like the back of her hand. She would point out spots on the green that appeared flat, but had a consistent break to them. She knew where all the good bailout spots were, which direction the wind was likely to be coming from, and what I could likely carry or not carry. She was extremely professional, but not cold. Whatever had transpired the evening before, whether there was something more to it or not, on this day we were more than player and caddy; we were friends. I loved every minute of it. Because of the nature of the round, as I said before many balls being played from a variety of positions, I cannot report a score but as I have already inferred, I was happy with my day's work.

After the round we went to the driving range for a short warm down. I was suddenly reminded of Melissa's expression of surprise that I knew she had been to the range on Saturday afternoon. The whole thing: me hitting the target, her hitting the target, repeatedly... had it been just a coincidence? Was she even aware I was hitting the target too? Was she not competing with me? I was too reticent to ask. But I was cocky enough to take out my eight-iron, take dead aim, and hit the same target on my first attempt. I looked at the ground so I could smile - no, *beam* – undetected. I was pretty chuffed. My relative smugness dissipated in an instant though, when I was brought back to reality by a loud *clang!* I looked up and Melissa was two stalls over, having taken a seven-iron from my bag and a half a dozen range balls. She swung again. *Clang!* I stared in awe as she turned, looked at me, and laughed like there was no tomorrow. *This*, if no other, was the moment I fell in love with Melissa Jones.

John Westley

Chapter ~~69~~ 12

I offered to make dinner. It was one thing for her to let me stay, another for her to caddy, yet another to become my emergency masseuse; the least I could do was make her dinner.

"I can't think the last time someone made me dinner," she said.

"Andy must have made you dinner?" Andy and I were on a first name basis.

"Ha!" she laughed. "Not on your life."

"Not once?" She shook her head. "Ever?" I asked, wide-eyed.

"Not even a sandwich," she answered. "Wait, that's not true, he did make me a sandwich once. Gave me a sandwich."

"Giving you a sandwich doesn't count, no more than buying you dinner. He has to *make* the sandwich," I declared.

"Oh," she said, "he made the sandwich. He just didn't like it, so he gave it to me," Melissa explained in a comical tone. I laughed.

"And was it a bad sandwich?"

"It was okay. He's just fussy."

"Or you're not," I added.

"Or I'm not. I'm really not, you know. I know it looks like I live a nice lifestyle, and I like what I have. But I don't need it. I have what I have because I could easily get it, not because I demanded or needed it. Especially now; what do I need a five bedroom house for?"

"It must be a lot to maintain," I suggested.

"Yes and no. There's only me here, so I don't wander around the house messing it up. I usually stick to two rooms, and I do confess a cleaner comes in once a week. But I don't need this. I'd rather have two smaller homes, one here and one somewhere warm."

"Now you're talking my language," I exclaimed. "My dream is to have a small place in Mexico."

Melissa beamed. "Mine too! Eight or nine months here, three or four months there, eating, drinking margaritas, and walking around in a bikini." Now it was my turn to beam, as I imagined Melissa in a bikini. It was not hard to imagine. I pictured her lying on the beach, tanned skin, white bikini, sipping her margarita as little beads of sweat appeared on her warm, smooth skin, amazed at their enviable luck. "So what are we having for dinner?" she asked. "Hello? I say, what are we having for dinner? Earth to Dan Green, come in Dan Green!" I snapped out of my daydream, but with no clue of what I had been asked. So, naturally, I said,

"What?"

"I asked what we are having for dinner." She smiled, and I suspect knew where I had been. After I collected myself I replied,

"Well, I'm not telling you what I'm making, but we do have to stop for a few things."

John Westley

"I did a pretty big grocery shop the other day, what do you need?"

"Oh, if I told you that it would give everything away."

"I say that as I may have what you need already," she added, digging.

"I'm pretty sure you don't," I countered, confidently at that.

***

Off to the grocery store we went.

We had both traveled in one car that day; hers. Melissa reasoned that it did not make sense to take two cars – fair enough – and as she knew the area it made the most sense for her to drive. I think she just could not stomach the thought of sitting in the Corolla Inn, replete with all the wonderful smells of a man having lived in it the past little while. We arrived at the store and suddenly I found myself in a scenario I certainly would never have imagined: pushing a shopping cart down the aisles of a supermarket with my caddy, who happened to be an insanely gorgeous and engaging woman.

"First thing I need is meat," I explained. "Bacon."

"I have tons of bacon at home," Melissa informed me. "So please don't."

"Cheese then," I continued.

"What kind?"

"You probably don't have it," I said.

"Try me."

Oh how I wanted to. "Cheddar," I said.

"Cheddar? Why it's the single most popular cheese in the world," Melissa quickly quipped… in an English accent… mimicking a line from the famous Monty Python cheese sketch. If I was not already in love with Melissa Jones, *that* would have been the moment I fell head over heels. (In the sketch, by the British comedy troupe *Monty Python,* John Cleese visits a cheese shop that boasts a wide variety of cheeses. However, every type of cheese Cleese requests is sold out, according to the shop clerk played by Michael Palin. Finally the Cleese character resorts to asking for 'cheddar' to which he is told the store does not carry cheddar, as there is no call for it. "But it's the single most popular cheese in the world!" cries Cleese.

"Not around here, sir," replies Palin.)

That Melissa had cited that line so quickly, and in a delicious British accent to boot, was almost too much for me to handle. My instinct was to grab her and kiss her hard on the lips, right there in dairy. I had to remind myself that whatever was going on here was professional. Even if between the lines there was something else going on – something romantic, something sexy – it was all too possible it was one way. That it all could be going on in my head was something I kept reminding myself, over and over. I knew that while I was fantasizing about ripping her form fitting clothes off and making love to her on the hardwood of her front hallway, she could be thinking that that was a good price for camembert.

"I have cheddar," Melissa clarified. "What next?" So far our shopping cart is empty."

"Pasta."

"Oh good. I was wondering where this was heading. But I have pasta."

"Not this kind," I stated confidently.

"You've been wrong before."

"Not this time," I chirped back, and pushed the cart further along to the pasta I spied on the other side of the aisle. "Come on," I added. Melissa smiled, and caught up with me.

"Okay, Galloping Gourmet, what is this pasta you think I don't have?"

"Close your eyes," I ordered. "This could be a little embarrassing." Enjoying the game, Melissa complied and closed her beautiful baby blues. Oh my god. She did not just close her eyes, but put her chin out and shoulders back. Her already perfect body now pronounced, noticing her exquisite form, the roundness of her breasts, became unavoidable. If ever there was an opportunity to steal a kiss that was it. But you know me by now; enough to know I became transfixed by the vision before me but too chicken-shit to steal the kiss. What I did do was reach out and, using my right hand, retrieved two boxes of Kraft Dinner from the store shelf and placed them in the shopping cart.

Anyone who is familiar with Kraft Dinner knows that you cannot move a box without making a very distinct sound akin to Mexican maracas. This sound prompted Melissa to open her eyes and spot what we were having for dinner.

"You've got to be kidding me," she exclaimed with good natured laughter. "*That* is what we are having for dinner?"

"Don't be so quick to judge, grasshopper," I suggested with a smile. "Bear with me; you won't be disappointed."

"You were right about one thing," she conceded. "I don't have any of *that* in my cupboards!"

"Trust me, after this dinner you will make a point to always stock a couple of boxes."

"Of wine?" she asked, sarcastically.

***

Wearing a kitchen apron of Melissa's that read *'Born to Golf Forced to Cook'* I set to work. Melissa poured us each a glass of cabernet and then sat herself upon the kitchen counter to witness my culinary skills, albeit with predictable skepticism. I started with bacon. She was right, bacon was not in short supply and I put it to good use. First I made a 'bacon weave' – laying strips of bacon both vertically and horizontally, weaving each piece over one and under another. I made two weaves and placed them, along with a few additional solo strips of bacon, on a pan. Before depositing them in the oven I added the key element. The sauce. A mixture of traditional barbecue sauce, hot sauce (I put that shit on everything) and… Jack Daniels. I painted on the sauce with the care of Picasso. Strike that, let's go with Jackson Pollock. (And yes, I did clean up afterward.) I deposited my creation into the oven and while what I had done was not difficult at all, Melissa feigned being impressed. I could live with feigned. I was having fun.

Melissa was having fun, also. I had just put water on to boil and when I turned around I caught her, still perched on the kitchen counter, taking a swig of JD. Seeing she had been caught she laughed, and almost spat the mouthful all over herself. With a mischievous grin she extended the bottle toward me, for me to have a go. She would not give me the bottle; I had to open my mouth as she poured. And as soon as I did, she pulled the bottle ever so slightly toward her, compelling me to follow. The next thing I knew I could feel her bare legs either side of me as my mid-section hit the counter.

I was beside myself. I was between her legs. So to speak. A rush shot through me affecting every artery and vein in my body. I was instantly hard and had to back away from the counter a little bit just to accommodate my sudden erection. I was dying to loosen my pants but had both hands firmly planted on the kitchen counter, either side of Melissa's incredible legs. Melissa pulled the bottle away from my mouth and took another swig with hers. She swallowed, and looked down at me, her eyes looking into mine with purpose. Not a word had been said. I could not have spoken if I wanted to.

For once I took the initiative and leaned in a little closer, worried she might back away. She did not. Her lips moist with remnants of whiskey, she leaned in about the same amount I had, closing the gap but a gap still existed. My eyes diverted from her wet lips to her rich blue eyes and locked in. She did not blink, just stared back into my eyes. It was now or never so I leaned in and put my hungry lips onto hers. We kissed. Hard. My hands moved to her bare thighs as she slid her body closer to mine and the intensity of the kiss grew. Finally Melissa pulled back some, looking a little hot and bothered as she said,

"Hmm, boiling."

"Mmmm, I'm hot too," I replied with a devilish grin.

"No, the water, on the stove, it's boiling." I had to think for a moment to even recall where

I was. Of course I was in Melissa's kitchen, and indeed the water for the macaroni was boiling, and bubbling over onto the stove. I moved toward the stove, then turned back to peek at Melissa for a moment - a 'pinch-me moment' - to make sure I was not imagining all this. I turned down the element heat, hoping this would not have a trickle down effect.

Coyly, with my back to her I said, "So once the water is boiling you add the macaroni, stirring as you do to avoid clumps. It is very important to avoid clumping." I turned back to face Melissa just as she slid off the counter landing squarely on her feet. I moved to her and we embraced like long lost lovers. Certainly not the same way most golfers hug their caddy. For the first time I could feel her chest, pressed up against me. Her breasts felt large, firm and amazing. I looked down and was further turned on by the vision of her cleavage. My right hand moved to her hair, running through it as we continued to kiss madly. Without conscious thought I gave her hair a little tug and she responded with a passionate moan. Note to self.

My mouth pressed firmer against hers as my left hand moved with a mind of its own to her ass. I squeezed. Her back arched. I hesitate to say her knees went weak, but I could feel the weight of her body in my arms as her legs ceased to support her. Slowly, ever so slowly, and without missing a beat of a kiss I lowered her to the kitchen floor.

This was no time to worry about stirring the noodles. There she lay beneath me, her back on the floor, knees raised, my body between them hovering above her. I lifted her a bit and slowly removed her shirt. I should not have been but I was surprised by how ripped her stomach was. My eyes moved from the tight muscles of her tummy to her now verifiably amazing breasts, packed into a black Victoria Secret bra. I do not know much about women's under garments, but I know my Victoria Secret. My mouth pulled my eyes away from her breasts as it moved to her mid-section. I began to methodically, no, passionately, kiss every square inch of it. Working from lower to upper tummy, savoring every moment of this once in a lifetime experience. My lips neared her breasts, heaving and still clothed, before beginning a return trip sliding down the solid ripples of her stomach. Down, down, and further down.

I could feel her tense in anticipation of where my mouth was headed, but I made her wait. This was too much fun. I felt her shorts with my chin, and then moved directly to her feet, kissing them, sucking gently on her toes. First one foot, then the other. I moved upward, my own excitement building in torrents as my lips met her firm right calf, my hand subtly tickling the back of her left thigh. I switched. Left calf, right thigh. My other hand, working independent of my brain, moved to Melissa's breasts as my mouth continued its pilgrimage north.

I was astonished that, insanely excited as I was, I felt in control. I had not been with a woman in a long while and by all rights could be forgiven if I had indeed lost it. Not by her, perhaps, but by those who could empathize. My only distraction was a conscious realization that this was what 'being in the moment' felt like. And despite the thought, I managed to stay in it.

I wanted Melissa so much, but also loved the excitement and anticipation I was experiencing. Added to my thrill was the increasing intensity and pace of her moans. Each 'Oh god' inspired my determination to please her to the full extent of my ability. Not at all unselfish as the more turned on she appeared to be, the more excited I became. I was reaching excitement levels never before imagined, not by me, anyway. A woman I was fantasizing about mere days ago was now half naked and lying beneath me on her kitchen floor. A woman, with Muppet headcovers.

My mouth finally reached its destination. Her body shook. I teased her with my tongue, circling, exploring, circling again, exploring some more. I had gone from wondering how she would react if I stole a kiss in a grocery store, to experiencing her reaction as I went down on her with a passion I did not know I possessed. This is not to say I was a crazy man; far from it. I felt calm and in control, while at the same time pleasantly light headed. It was as if I had a buzz on, though I knew it was not from the small amount of Jack Daniels that had entered my system. No, Melissa Jones had entered my system and I was intoxicated because of it. Because of her.

I do not know how many times she uttered the words before it registered, but I suddenly became aware of the need to listen. I focused, and she repeated them, "I want you."

"I want you too," I replied, honestly.

"Inside me." Those words echoed through my brain as my hands moved to her shorts. Her hands were already there, trying to slip them off despite her position on the floor beneath me. Her tantalizing stomach muscles tightened as together we slid her shorts down her tanned legs, and over her milk white feet. My hands returned to her waist in search of her undies. None were to be found. Only the bra remained and my hands slid beneath her back, prompting Melissa to say, "The front." I looked, and the clasp was indeed at the front, between her seemingly now larger breasts. Brilliant. I undid her bra with ease (a godsend) and both sides flung open, exposing her perfect breasts. Real, and yes, fabulous.

I sat up and managed not to panic as I unbuckled my jeans. I used the opportunity to cast a long glance over her alluring body, scanning from head to toe as I lowered my pants to my knees. As much as I knew she wanted me inside, and as much as I wanted and needed to enter her, I leaned forward as my mouth moved to her breasts and devoured them with kisses. Kissing uninterrupted, I was so hard it was not at all difficult to find her warmth and begin to enter her. Begin, being the key word. This was too good and too long in coming to just drive inside and, surely, explode. I entered her, but just a tiny bit, playing with her with the tip. Then I stopped all playing. I paused. Just inside her but undoubtedly part of her now, I stopped where I was and looked at Melissa. Her eyes met mine, longingly but it was more than that. I was not in the mood to debate my own instincts, there was clearly a connection here. Her eyes, my eyes, communicating as nothing else happened. Nothing else, until I slid suddenly and deeply inside her. She gasped. Her back arched. My back arched, as I strove to be a part of her as deeply as my body could enable.

Melissa's body shuddered; there is no better word to describe it. Trembled does not cut it, although it describes me perfectly after finally releasing and exploding. I had never experienced orgasm like that before, and that she came with me intensified the experience in unknown multitudes. I collapsed on top of her only to feel her arms and legs, wrap around me as we embraced. My eyes caught hers just for a flash before I lowered my mouth to hers, and we kissed. A long, sustained kiss, which was almost as brilliant as the entire experience preceding it. I knew better than to use the 'love' word immediately after sex, even if – no, especially if – only to myself. But that was what it felt like. Then, and only then, did I wonder if the noodles had boiled over too.

Chapter ~~69~~ 13

To say the nature of our conversation over dinner had changed would be an understatement. Oh, we had dinner. The noodles were not al dente but everything else was fine. We ended up eating from bowls, right there on the kitchen floor. Side by side, backs leaning against the cupboards, her left leg draped over my right one. Our pillow talk? Swing theory. Yes, golf swing theory. Whether it was to mask a nervousness about our intimacy, or whether we needed to be intimate before talking about such a sensitive topic, I cannot say for sure. Melissa wanted to know what my trip to Tofino was all about, and what I had learned.

"Hit Down Dammit!" I said.

"What?" Melissa asked with a laugh. I explained that the instructor in Tofino had written a book called *Hit Down Dammit!* It was the first instruction book that actually made logical sense to me. So much so that I committed a month of my life to letting the guy repeat over and over what I had already read in the book. But apparently that was what I needed, repetition was what I got, and I drove out of there in my Toyota Corolla a changed man. As was evidenced that night, although I did not mention that part.

I went on to explain the theory, and she asked all the same questions I had when I first arrived in Tofino. Her questions were intelligent, and showed she had more than a cursory understanding of the golf swing. The problem was her understanding, as mine had been, was heavily influenced by custom rather than logic.

"I love that you are willing to talk about this with me," Melissa said as she put her arm on mine.

"Are you kidding? I'm thrilled *you* are willing to talk about this sort of stuff. My ex used to refer to golf as *'the G word'* and would not tolerate any discussion of it. The funny thing is she was an equestrian."

"Why is that funny?" Melissa asked.

"Because," I said, "I helped her with her horses regularly. It was okay for me to shovel shit out of stalls, but she could not talk about my round for five minutes."

"So you could shovel shit, but she didn't give a shit, is what you are saying," Melissa said in a brilliantly comical tone. I burst out laughing and had no hesitation in leaning forward to give her a kiss. "Andy would never talk swing theory with me," Melissa continued. "He argued that it would confuse his own mechanics, yet I would see him talking about it with fellow pros on the range every day."

"You have a beautiful swing," I told her. "I assumed you got that by working with Andy?"

"First, I don't have a beautiful swing, but thank you. And nope, didn't get an ounce of help from Andy. But I did get to watch some of the best swings in the world over and over, so I like to think osmosis helped. Even on the mini tours, which is when I caddied for Andy the most, you get to see incredibly beautiful golf swings. They are just not all attached to brains that can win. I'm sure you've seen that."

"I hope I'm not that," I confessed. Quickly Melissa countered,

"Oh you're not that. You have a winner's brain, it didn't take long to see that on Monday." I was stunned.

"I've already made you dinner," I said. "And let you have your way with me. As reluctant as I was. You don't have to butter me up." Melissa feigned offence as she responded exuberantly,

"I'm not buttering you up! I know a winner when I see one and I saw one on Monday. No, on Saturday in fact. How can you not know that?"

"I guess I never saw myself that way," I again confessed. Confession was indeed becoming good for the soul. "I always thought I had a pretty decent game, and it was my head getting in the way."

"Well maybe your head was just fine, and it was your game that needed fine-tuning. And this guy in Tofino did that. Think about it, if you didn't have a winner's attitude you may never have bothered to go to Tofino in the first place. But from what I saw, especially on Monday, you have what it takes. To get to the next level at least." I kept finding new ways to fall in love with Melissa and I did again, sitting there on her kitchen floor.

We went to bed; her bed. I would love to say we made mad passionate love all night long, but the truth is we spooned. We talked for a bit longer, but we were both clearly tired and there was still reality to deal with. The next day was the pro-am. Pro-ams are an annoyance to some, as I alluded to earlier, but they are also an opportunity to make some cash. While the prize money did not rival what would be doled out at the four day tournament, a good finish at the pro-am could cover one's expenses for the week and lighten the pressure going into round one. I do not even know when we fell asleep. And I did not care. All I knew was that I adored the feeling of her naked body before mine, my arms wrapped around her, legs intertwined, falling asleep a winner.

Chapter ~~69~~ 14

Everything in the world felt right as sun streamed in through Melissa's bedroom window the next morning. Her room was on the opposite side of the house to the room I had slept in the night before, and as such glowed from the luminance. All that was missing was Melissa. Not for long though, as she entered the room, fully dressed, carrying a coffee for me. I did actually pinch myself.

"Rise and shine, you have work to do today Mr. Green."

I smiled and said not a word as she handed me the mug of coffee. She left the room and I rose to get dressed. The only problem? This was not my room, and the clothes I had on the day before were likely still in the kitchen. They were not in Melissa's room. Funny how we can perform incredibly intimate acts one moment, and the next be tiptoeing self consciously down a corridor, stealing oneself for embarrassment if caught in the buff by the person we were intimate with in the first place. I made it though, got dressed, and went to the kitchen.

Eggs Benny awaited me, made by Melissa. All conversation was limited to the activities of the day ahead of us, and we soon departed for the golf course, and the pro-am. I had played in over a hundred tournaments, yet this day felt 'new' to me. As if I was playing for the first time. A tiny bit of nervousness but mixed with a quiet confidence. The confidence stemmed from my new faith in my game, and perhaps just as much my new state of mind. I really could go out and shoot a hundred and not care. I was blissfully happy for once. I reasoned that my bliss made it less likely I would go out and shoot a big number. It was a nice feeling.

We checked in at registration which is where we found out who the amateurs paired with me were going to be.

"Oh no," Melissa said as she looked at the pairing sheet. I did not know anyone on it, so I was in the dark, but *'Oh no'* are not exactly words you like coming from your caddy's mouth.

"What's wrong?" I asked.

"Nothing, really it's nothing."

"Come on," I said. "Spill." Melissa moved away from the registration tent and spoke quietly as she said,

"It's just you are paired with three of the most annoying women at the club," Melissa declared.

"Oh," I said, thinking for a moment. "Is it really that bad?"

"Hopefully not," Melissa replied. Not a great vote of confidence, but as I said I was in a great frame of mind and ready to take on anything that came my way. "Kimmi, Sandi, and

Tori. Known as the *Three I's* as each of their names ends with an i. They are in the Business Ladies division, always play together, always argue, and always swear to never play together again."

"But they always do, right?" I guessed.

"Right! It drives everyone crazy. I don't know how the pros put up with them."

"Because they have to."

"I suppose."

"Do their husbands have money?"

"Husbands? Two of them are LSL's and the other is a slut. She's single," Melissa added.

I was confused. "I know what a slut is, but you lost me with 'LSL'."

"Lipstick Lesbos. Lesbians."

"Lipstick Lesbians? Is that another kind?"

"They're lesbians, but they don't look it. In fact, they're very feminine looking, gorgeous. Just makes them even less likeable."

"Good point. I for one am only attracted to butt-ugly people, so have no fear."

"Oh you know what I mean," Melissa said while half-whacking me with her hand.

"And the slut?"

"Gorgeous. They're all three gorgeous. And all three certifiable."

"Dare I ask what they do for a living? I'm guessing they have some money; pro-ams aren't a cheap ticket.

"One's a lawyer, her partner does nothing, and the slut is a dentist."

"Gotta love a slut dentist," I joked.

"The funny thing is," Melissa continued, I think without hearing my remark at all, "I bet you it will take nine holes for you to even figure out which two are the couple."

I laughed. "You know, I do like to bet."

"Five bucks," Melissa offered.

I went for it. "You're on." I mean, how hard could it be, right?

***

Fast forward to the first tee. Yes I warmed up, hit balls, putted, chipped, the usual routine and Melissa was a trooper. A professional, I should say. She really was a first rate caddy and even after our explosive evolution in relationship she took no liberties, taking her caddying duties seriously and I felt extremely well supported. We arrived at the tee in time to watch the group ahead of us tee off, on time. I loved it when a tee ran on time, especially on pro-am day when rounds could get up into the range of five hours. A tee that was running a half hour late usually meant the length of the round would go up exponentially.

I recognized the pro in the group ahead. Frank Brentlin, or Brently, something like that. A Texan. Similar to this day, I had been in the pro-am group behind him at a tournament in California. He was introduced to his three pro-am partners, your typicals… doctors, lawyers, brokers, in that vein. And he gave them 'the speech':

"Look, I'm happy to play with you and all, but I have to tell you this. For you this is a day out, a lark. For me, this is my work. I play golf for a living and I have to concentrate. I don't have time to answer your questions, give you swing tips, chit chat about your grandkids, none of it. So play your game, keep your distance, and whatever you do, don't talk to me." The three amateurs stood there with their mouths hanging open, thinking *'We paid two grand for this?'* As they stood in dumbfounded amazement Frank reached into his gigantic tour bag, pulled out four cans of Bud, handed one to each of them and said, "Now, who wants a beer?" A very funny guy, one of the highlights of the mini-tour circuit.

But by the time Frank and his partners were out of range on this given day, it was still Melissa and me standing on the first tee, partner-less.

"I'm sorry, Mr. Green," the starter said as he approached me. "We kinda gotta give them a couple more minutes."

"That's okay," I said, just as three bickering female voices could be heard coming from the direction of the cart path. I had to laugh as the three of them came over the horizon, the visual belying the aural. Visually they looked like the opening credits of Charlie's Angels. Three stupidly gorgeous women walking side by side, guns replaced by drivers, their hair bouncing like a Revlon commercial. Hell, their hair even matched the Angels, with two brunettes book-ending one blonde.

But to listen to them, you would swear you were in Target listening to three women fight over the last handbag on Black Friday. They were all three speaking at the same time, so I could only make out random lines like *"If you'd only listened"* and *"Do you mind, I'm talking!"* Sufficient to say it only took about 1.7 seconds to see why Melissa had said *"Oh no"* when she saw who I was paired with. The next order of the day was to figure out which one was the straight one, er, I mean the dentist. They walked straight past the starter, ignored Melissa completely, and strutted directly up to me. Smiles suddenly appeared as if someone had hit a switch.

"You must be Dan Green," one of the brunettes began.

"I'm Kimmi Farwell," the other brunette said, jumping in.

"I'm Tori Torbet," the blonde chimed in.

"I'm sorry, I didn't get your name," I said to the first brunette.

"No you didn't," she replied, casting a mean glance at Kimmi. "I'm Sandi

Hollingsworth." Wow, Kimmi, Tori, and Sandi; this was going to be hard to keep straight. Not that someone named *Dan* could complain. And no, I would not be changing my name to *Dani* anytime soon.

"Sorry to keep you waiting, Mr. Green, we'll quickly tee off and then we can get on with what is sure to be a wonderful day." Before the word *day* was out of Sandi Hollingsworth's mouth, Kimmi Farwell had her ball teed in the ground and was about to hit when interrupted by the rather overshadowed starter.

"Excuse me, Miss-" he began.

"Ms. Farwell," Ms. Farwell said interrupting, putting emphasis on the *Ms.*

The starter tried again. "I'm sorry, Ms. Farwell, but Mr. Green tees first, from the black tees, and then you three ladies will tee from the red tees."

"Who are you calling a lady?" Tori burst out, sending all three women (Melissa excluded) into fits of laughter – apparently the humor of this remark being something the three could actually agree on.

"We did not pay two thousand dollars each to play from the red tees," Kimmi declared.

"Did the group in front of us play from the red tees?" Sandi asked.

"Well, ah, no," the starter answered honestly, if not confidently.

114

"Then why must we?" Tori asked. The poor starter, he was dead. They were dying for him to say it, daring him to say it. He tried the back door.

"Well, that group was all men."

"So?" the three responded in unison. The second thing they had agreed on thus far. Progress.

"Oh, whatever," the starter said, his arm dropping and his clipboard banging his thigh as he turned and walked away. I looked over at Melissa who was attempting to bury her head in one of the bigger pockets of my tour bag feigning a search for something in order to hide her unavoidable laughter.

Ms. Farwell then teed off and I have to say hit a pretty decent shot. That said, the black tees for professionals are a *long* way back on these kinds of golf courses, quite a bit further back than the traditional "back tees" for members who are considered low handicappers. So as decent as her shot was, it rolled to a stop about fifty yards beyond the – you guessed it – red tees. Sandi was next. She hit a much higher drive that carried further than Kimmi's, but rolled much less, ending up almost equidistant. Tori then took a wild swing, as if inspired by the pressure to hit well beyond the red tees, and sliced the ball into a lateral hazard to the right. She ended up being quite generous to herself in her estimation of the point of entry into said

John Westley

hazard, and took a drop remarkably close to the golf balls of her counterparts.

By all rights I should have teed off first, but I wisely kept my mouth shut, swung back, hit down, and torched a drive down the right side of the fairway. Perfection would have had it draw back to the center, but I was not complaining. I was thrilled in fact; I appeared to own this swing. Less than perfect, but perfectly useful.

***

Melissa was the model of professionalism. She knew these women yet through three holes not one of them had acknowledged her, let alone say hello. For the most part she stuck close to me, which made my day anyway, and she went about her business. But at other times she would walk on ahead to scope what lay before me, or to take my clubs to the next tee, and let the Angels chat and flirt with me. It was all water off a duck's back. Little did I realize how well the duck analogy fit. We all know about the duck that appears to be calm, above the water surface.

Of course I had been warned about my playing partners by Melissa, and while they were even *more* larger-than-life than I was expecting I was okay with it. What did surprise me was a sudden change in the barometric pressure. In a matter of an hour you could feel the air change as storm clouds moved in, something I had begun to think did not exist in Heaven. It was almost a relief from the humidity that had been in the air, but no golfer likes the threat of rain. Especially one that is two under through five holes. The sky grew a little darker but remained that way for quite some time, giving hope that we might get our round in before the 'heavens' opened.

I had not forgotten my task, to determine by the ninth hole which of the three ladies were a couple, and which was in the medical profession. It actually served as a useful sidebar to keep me from getting overly carried away with how well I was playing, and from thinking too much about what might occur at Melissa's once we got home. I thought it would be a cakewalk to determine which two people, out of just three, were in love. It was no cakewalk and I could see why Melissa was prepared to put five bucks down. All three were flirts, first of all. Not just with each other, which was bizarre enough, but with me in particular. But all three were at each other just as often; incessantly in fact,

'You're swinging too fast!'
'Do you have to stand there?'
'You're annoying the pro.'
'No I'm not!' (said loudly enough to annoy the pro two holes over.)
'Can I borrow your nine-wood?'
'You're not allowed to borrow clubs!'

John Westley

'You are if you don't have fourteen! Isn't that right, Dan?' This last one put me in the awkward position of having to get involved,

"Well, technically you are a team so you can give a club to a team-mate provided they have less than fourteen clubs, but, they are not allowed to give it back to you."

"See!" Kimmi said.

"That's ridiculous, why can't you give it back?" Sandi demanded to know.

"It's to prevent a team of three, like yourselves, having 39 total clubs and trading back and forth constantly," I tried to quickly explain.

"Oh," Sandi replied. Tori then whispered to Sandi,

"I don't think I understand."

Sandi whispered back, "Neither do I."

Tori: "Can I borrow your nine-wood?"

"No," Sandi replied.

***

It was probably a good thing – indeed, it was a good thing – that I found the antics of the three so amusing. Annoying would be the alternative, and annoying mixes with golf like oil and water. I did start to notice, however, that Melissa, while quiet in the first place, was becoming more and more aloof. I tried to ask if she was okay and I got that classic answer, "I'm fine," said in a tone that implied not fine at all.

Men should not be allowed to use the word *fart* and women should not be allowed to use the word *fine*. But I digress.

Of course, none of the Three I's had caddies. Still Melissa remained steadfastly focused on me, not because she was unwilling to help the others, I do not think, but more out of a professional loyalty to the person who was paying her. Not that I had yet paid her a dime, nor had we even talked money. We had been busy talking about other things. Melissa clearly wanted to help me do well this week, and her professionalism was unwavering. However there was one instance when Melissa found Sandi's ball, saving her from an almost sure-fire lost ball penalty. This also marked the first time *any* of the three women spoke to Melissa that day.

"Oh, you found my ball?" Sandi asked.

"Yes, it is over there," Melissa stated, pointing toward a clump of grass adjacent to the trunk of a tree.

"Thank you."

"You're welcome."

"How are you, Melissa?"

"I'm fine."

"That's good to hear," Sandi stated. "You look good. Time away seems to have agreed with you. Oh dear, where is my ball again?"

"Over there," Melissa replied tersely, again pointing, while walking back toward me with a very annoyed grimace on her beautiful face. At this precise time, Tori bizarrely grabbed hold of my arm.

"My, what strong arms you have, Mr. Green."

"Dan, please," I said, embarrassed, even more so with Melissa approaching.

"I guess it's from all that swinging," Tori added. She of the three had been the most flirtatious that day, but this was taking it to another, more peculiar level.

While Tori's actions were more overt, it seemed Melissa was more annoyed with Sandi. I had no idea what was going on, aside from the fact I knew Melissa did not care for these women. But she seemed more acutely upset now, despite her best efforts to be professional and support me. I was - naively perhaps - assuming these three women knew nothing of the relationship developing between Melissa and me. How could they? We had just met the other day, we had been extremely professional at the golf club, and all our other developments had been behind her closed doors. One breakfast out had been the limit to our non-golf-club, non-closed-doors activity and it had seemed innocuous enough. I know Heaven is a small town; I come from a small town, so I get the whole small town mentality stuff. But no way one breakfast out, the week a big golf event is in town, a golf pro and his caddy having breakfast could conjure anything up. Right?

***

In the meantime, the sky had come out of its holding pattern and was darkening, coupled with an ominous sound far off in the distance. The sound of thunder. Not good. Indeed it was only about five minutes later another ominous sound could be heard, that of the lightning warning horn. This golf club's was more of a siren, and there was no mistaking it. It apparently upset the gods above Heaven as loud crackles of thunder replied in earnest.

"What's that?" Tori asked, to which Melissa, speaking for almost the first time, replied quickly,

"It's your car alarm." The other two just howled, and Tori joined in half-heartedly presumably for fear of appearing like she did not get the joke.

"It's the lightning warning, silly," Kimmi explained.

"It's telling us to come in," I added.

"Do we have to?" Sandi asked.

"I'm going in," Tori said. "I don't want to get hit by lightning again."

"You've never been hit by lightning," Kimmi said with a tone.

"Have too, when I was little."

"That would explain a lot," Sandi said sarcastically.

"When and where?" Kimmi asked.

"I don't remember," Tori replied. "On account of the lightning."

"Well that's convenient," Kimmi added, again in a tone.

The three were still bickering when a multi-passenger golf cart arrived, impressively promptly, to drive us back in to the safety of the clubhouse. Everyone got in but Melissa just deposited my clubs in the back, and said something about walking in.

"Melissa, jump on, we're a long way out," I suggested.

"There's not enough room," came her reply, somewhat tersely.

"Sure there is, you can even sit on my lap," I said with a smile as I too got into the cart.

"It's okay, I'll walk; I know a shortcut." With that Melissa turned and walked toward the forest just as the rain began. And it began with a bang. The driver of the golf cart wasted no time pulling away as he no doubt had several return trips to make. Seeing Melissa was serious about walking in I leapt off the cart, telling the driver to go on without me. I was not sure, but I thought I heard one of the women say,

"He's so in love with her," as the cart departed. I darted toward the forest in pursuit of my beloved caddy, wondering to myself what had sparked that comment given how aloof Melissa had been all morning. Or was that indeed the reason?

"Melissa!" I called out as I jogged to catch up to her and the rain continued to dump.

"You should've rode in," Melissa said as I reached her. "You'll get soaked."

"So will you," I pointed out.

"Ya, but I'm not playing in the tournament," she pointed out in turn.

"What's wrong?" I asked. "And please don't say you're fine."

"Nothing's wrong."

"That's the same as saying you're fine," I stated. "Something's up, what is it?"

"Just those women."

"Well, we knew they were annoying, you were right about that."

"They didn't seem to be annoying you."

"Nothing could annoy me, right now."

"What do you mean *'right now'*? Melissa asked.

"Are you kidding?"

"No, I'm not kidding. What do you mean?"

I grabbed Melissa by the shoulders, stopped her from continuing on what had become a torrid pace through the woods, and turned her to face me. Both of us were already dripping wet, but that was inconsequential. I decided not to mince words and get straight to the heart of the matter. "Nothing can annoy me *because of you.*"

Melissa looked at the ground, where streams of water running off of our golf caps struck each of our feet. "What do you mean *because of me*?" I remained patient.

"I have no idea what is going on here," I began, "but I do know that I am feeling things inside me *I have never felt*. And it has been *not* since going to Tofino, but since I saw you walk onto that practice range on Saturday. These past few days, regardless of what happens in the next few, have been the best of my life and with that, with the feelings I have for you, absolutely nothing could annoy me. I could start to shank the ball and I would still be smiling."

"You shouldn't use that word," Melissa said with the first hint of a smile in some while.

"You mean *feelings*?" I asked, even though I knew the joke she was making.

"No, I mean shank," she said, finishing off the punch line.

"Now *you* just said it."

"Damn, I did, didn't I?"

"Don't do it again," I said as I placed my hand under her soft feminine chin and gently tilted her head until her eyes met mine. Even in the forest rain was coming down steadily as I moved my mouth towards hers and kissed her. She threw her arms around my neck and pulled herself up into the kiss. I kissed her harder, inadvertently pushing her back, up against a tree, as I kissed her passionately. Her response was incredible, just as passionate, a level of passion beyond what we had experienced the night before. I lifted her up and her legs wrapped around me as we continued to kiss madly. I stepped back, pulling her away from the tree and we stood in the middle of the forest, me holding Melissa, her clinging to me. I dropped to my knees as we continued to kiss, and then laid her back down on the wet ground. Simultaneously I unbuckled my pants as she went for her shorts and slid them down to her knees. My head went dizzy as I entered her. Her gasp was other worldly. I drove deep, she responded pushing her tummy into the air. My hands moved to her ass to support her, and to attempt to be a part of her as deep as I possibly could. We both screamed an uninhibited scream and then collapsed to the ground. Soaking wet man on top of soaking wet woman, still united. Still hugging. Still kissing. I had never experienced such a moment in my life, and doubted I ever would again. My attitude toward pro-ams would never be the same.

Chapter ~~69~~ 15

Very wet, even dirtier, and feeling good Melissa and I slunk back to the clubhouse and in. I always carried a change of clothes when playing in tournaments, and Melissa of course had a locker so getting cleaned up and changed was not a big issue. One person did ask me what happened, when they saw me drenched and covered in dirt, but I just said I fell walking in and their delight at this outweighed any skepticism. So I was good.

What was an issue was what the tournament organizers were to do about their pro-am. Pro-ams are tricky business; there is no tomorrow because the professional tournament must start on time. Canceling is not easy as there are usually well over a hundred people who paid two grand to play. They are not going to go home quietly.

Also a factor, even if the weather bounces back (or especially if the weather bounces back) is the pro-am dinner. A lot of work - and food - goes into a pro-am dinner, and to many the dinner is as big a deal as the golf. To the amateurs that is. Most of the pros could care less. That is not quite true; many of the pros do care. They resent being forced to go to the dinner with the thinking that they could be practicing, or getting an early night before the first day of competition. Ask anyone with a 7:00 am tee time. So there they sit, surrounded by amateurs at a ratio of at least three to one, nowhere to hide, no excuse for not answering questions.

The have-not pros see a silver lining in the free meal provided. The very big free meal. The all-you-can-eat free meal. The industrious pros recognize that many pro-am dinners are attended by half the local town's millionaires and if they can put on a good show – both on and off the course – they could potentially find themselves a sponsor. Not a sponsor in the widely accepted sense of a Nike, or a Titleist, but a wealthy business man or woman who might advance them a cool 50 grand to cover their expenses for a season. Even a mini-tour pro can drop 50 in a year quite easily. Between travel, be it by plane or car (usually the latter), hotels and motels (usually the latter), food, clothes, tour fees and entry fees, caddies' wages, and who knows what else, it does not take long.

You can always tell the pros that have wealthy benefactors – they dress better, look more rested, kibitz more on the driving range, and generally have more hair. This is of course thanks to the significantly reduced stress associated with not having to worry about how you are going to fill your car with gas. Even a Corolla.

Typically a sponsorship like this will last just one season, so it is up to the pro to make the most of it. The goal is to use the free ride to play well and win enough money to become self-sufficient for the following season. For one year the fifty thousand gives the backer bragging rights that they "have a golf pro" but that novelty has pretty much dried up by the time a second check is needed.

A great sponsor-related story is of Champions Tour star Kenny Perry. In his younger days Perry had failed in his first two attempts to qualify for the PGA Tour at Q-school. He missed by one stroke one year and received word that his wife had gone into labor during the fourth round the next year. He had been sponsored by a group of about twenty individuals, many local citizens from Franklin, Kentucky in his early play on the mini-tours and his first two attempts at the annual qualifying tournament. In 1985, a local businessman lent him five thousand dollars for another shot at qualifying. Instead of repay the loan, Perry was asked to give five percent of his tour earnings to Lipscomb University if he qualified. What they did not quite imagine was that Perry would go on to win 22 tournaments and earn over 35 million dollars in prize money in what turned out to be a long and successful career. Even though he was let out of his obligation to donate five percent, Perry has insisted on maintaining the deal to this day and still funds a scholarship for local residents to attend the university.

But I digress.

The tournament organizers came up with an ingenious plan I had never seen done before. Bearing in mind the fact players were teeing off both the front and back nines that morning, they were able to determine that almost everyone in the field had played holes one through fifteen, or ten through six by the time play halted. In the anticipation that there would be some chance to play at least a few more holes, the day's results would be based on team score on holes one to six and ten to fifteen combined. For players who had managed to get their full round in prior to rain, only those holes would count from their scorecards and they had the added benefit of remaining in the bar. Teams who had played at least one through six and ten through fifteen had the option of returning to the links for more golf, or remaining in the bar to drink their faces off. To encourage pros to return to the course and not let their teams down, a "skins" pot was created where only an eagle could win. ("Skins" is where only the single lowest score from the entire field on a single hole can win. For instance, if you score a two on say the sixth hole, if no one in the field can match your two on that hole you win all the money in the skins pot. If another player also bests the field on yet a different hole, they too win a skin and the skins pot would be divided between the two of you.)

As hoped the weather did break, and there was a mass exodus back to the golf course to play as many holes as could be squeezed in before 6:30 p.m. with dinner pushed back to 7:00. The pros more than cooperated and thanks to the skins pot they put on a show. Not as worried about an overall score, they began taking more chances, put more into their drives, got bolder on their approach shots. I do not know whether I am proud or ashamed to say that I was not one of them.

Oh, our team went back out and played; but if there was one thing - and there were many - I learned from the instructor in Tofino it was to never, ever, stray from my game plan. He would joke, aptly, that only golfers would attempt a multitude of different ways to be consistent. "Only *being* consistent can breed consistency," he would say. And things were going far too well for me to mess with what was so clearly working.

We were one of the teams that just needed to complete one hole to be able to enter a score for the tournament, and then whatever golf we got in before 6:30 was just for fun. And skins. I did nearly make an eagle that could have won a skin, but it lipped out and I was certainly not the only pro on the course to have a putt lip out that day. But I *was* the only pro on the course having amazing sex with his caddy. Not that I can categorically prove that. Despite the shenanigans of my three playing partners we did manage to finish the eighteenth in time which meant a short walk to the clubhouse, and I did get to enter an eighteen-hole score, for pride sake. Despite being minus two after five, I was only minus three after eighteen having added two more birdies and a bogey. Another 69, and I stayed true to the promise to myself that I would never reject a 69. 69's were good.

What was not good, and that I had not even considered, was that caddies are not typically invited to pro-am dinners. The thought of attending the dinner without Melissa was abhorrent to me. The thought of me alone with the three I's was also abhorrent to me, but the lesser issue. Luckily Melissa was both a member of the golf club, and the ex-wife of golf star, Andy Jones. It is a little sad to see benefit to who someone's ex-husband is, but there was something fun about his notoriety, if I must confess. My mind did stray to wondering how many doors it might open, as opposed to close. But I also knew not to get ahead of myself. Play the hole I am currently on. For want of a better expression. The bottom line was Melissa was able to secure a ticket to the dinner, albeit at a different table. However good fortune persisted and one of the group we were seated with at a table for eight had to leave to deliver a baby (she looked visibly annoyed) opening a spot up with me and the rest of my team.

There I sat, with another pro from Canada and six pretty darned good looking women -

eclectic as they were - the envy of the room. Now, if I could just stop the women from killing each other.

Chapter ~~69~~ 16

It was at the bar (where else?) that I learned a vital piece of information that started to piece some things together. The information came courtesy of a local pro, whom I had never met before. But he was quite comfortable addressing me as we both lined up to order drinks.

"You're a brave man," the pro – whose name I never did learn – said. I was surprised to hear the word *'brave'* in place of *'lucky'* given the vision of my tablemates.

"Why's that?" I asked, nonchalantly.

"Well, you know who you're sitting with, right?"

"Sure, my team from today."

"And?"

"And my caddy."

"Pretty good looking caddy."

"She may be, but how does that make me brave?"

"Know who she is?" he asked. Suddenly I could see where this was going. Or so I thought.

"I do actually."

"Andy Jones' ex-wife."

"I said I do. Know, that is."

"Figured you did," he explained. "But do you know who else you are sitting with?"

"From the other team?" I wondered.

"From your team."

John Westley

"Sure, a lawyer, a dentist, and a something or other, not sure what she does."

"Well let's just say one of them is pretty damned familiar with Andy Jones' dental records."

I laughed. "So she's Jones' dentist?"

"Oh, she's more than his dentist," the pro blabbed.

"What do you mean?"

"Let's just say she gives him treatment that insurance doesn't cover."

"You're kidding?" I said, now intrigued. More than intrigued.

"She's the one that busted them up."

"Him and his wife?"

"It was the town joke, that she never knew. Until one day she saw them on TV together! Idiot dentist was following him in the gallery at the PGA in Seattle, and they got busted smooching."

"I remember that - holy crap I never would have made the connection though!" *Why would I?* To me Andy Jones was just another famous PGA Tour pro to envy prior to that week. Oh, poor Melissa, no wonder she was put off seeing who I was paired with. And she had more or less kept it together all day; all long, wet day. And now I had left her sitting at a table with the woman who slept with her husband. The only upside was I now knew for sure which of the three was the slut, but too late to collect my five bucks. Not that I would have the nerve.

After getting drinks I sat back down at our table and glanced across at Melissa. Thankfully she was talking to one of the women from the other team seated with us. She had moved chairs to join a conversation, while the Three I's talked animatedly about some new venture Kimmi was starting. I garnered that Sandi, the lawyer, was the breadwinner of the two and that Kimmi was prone to embarking on new business ventures that were not always very well thought through. I heard reference to a luxury quilt business, where bed covers went at 5k a pop, she sold two, and was then stuck with a hundred grand in covers that Sandi had to, well, cover.

Needless to say, my eye did not stray far from Melissa and I never ceased to get a kick out of hers catching mine. I had always associated beautiful women with a sense of insecurity – either theirs or mine. What was so nice here was she had a way of making me feel present, and confident. Typically I knew of two kinds of couples, and had only ever heard of a third. The *'get a room'* couple who are on each other like velcro, and the couple that enter a room and head for separate corners, never to intermingle again until the car ride home. If then. But you hear about – albeit in romantic, fanciful conversations about what love ought to feel like - the couple who can be on opposite sides of the room, or in separate conversations, but *feel* together. With a knowing glance, a wink of an eye, a hand gently brushing the other's backside as they pass by. I had never known, or experienced, that third type and sadly had equated it with the notion of World Peace, a cure for the common cold, or a Chicago Cubs' Series win.

Finally Melissa's conversation ended and she found the opportunity to move back to sit with me.

"Hi," she said. One word, so sweet.

"I'm sorry," I said.

"What on earth for?"

I gulped. "I heard what happened. Tori. And Andy."

"Oh," she replied. "Water under the bridge."

"I don't think so. And I'm sorry you had to put up with them all day today; I had no idea."

"Of course you didn't. And besides, we had a job to do, and still have a job to do. You're playing well and I think you have a chance." As she said those words I felt her leg brush up against mine, sending shivers and more throughout me. She leaned in close and whispered in my ear, "What are your thoughts on incredible sex the night before a tournament?" Blood rushed to parts of my body I need not mention.

69 Shades of Green: 7 Days in Heaven

"I don't know," I said, trying to be coy. Not sure if I was successful. "I haven't had much experience with it."

"Well, I am not going to force it on you," she said, coyly. She was successful.

"Why not?" I asked with a smile.

"I am serious about wanting you to do well this week. If I tire you out and it affects your play, I would feel horrible."

"Horrible?"

"Positively."

"But what if it improved my play?"

"Then I should think we would have to implement it into your routine."

"Not my pre-shot routine?"

"Well, yes, if possible; but I don't think that would be practical."

"Good point." Just then Melissa's foot, sans shoe, moved to an area between my legs with profound effect.

"God, I hope that was you," I said with a laugh.

"Can I ask you a question?" Melissa asked while penetrating my brain with her pupils.

"Of course."

"Why are we still here?"

"Another good point. I really should be getting to bed early tonight, shouldn't I?"

"You do have to play tomorrow." Her foot pushed on me once more. I had heard – and felt – enough. "Let's go," I affirmed. And we did.

***

We were already madly kissing as Melissa tried to unlock the front door. Emphasis on *tried,* as I am afraid I was no help despite it being in my interest to get her inside. I had her unashamedly pinned against the door as my lips pressed against hers, my torso against hers, her leg wrapped around mine and I had zero inclination to hide how inclined I was.

I of course had been turned on by pretty women before, but Melissa, she took me to another level that skipped levels I could not count. Intoxicating was how turned on *she* appeared to be. Each moan, each attack of my lips with hers, raised my arousal to heights I had no idea I possessed. Any man – on the planet – would have surely forgiven me had I climaxed prematurely, probably saying, *"Ya, can't blame him"*. I am not sure any woman on the planet would be so understanding, Melissa included, but what added to the surreal nature of my contact with this gorgeous creature was the fact I felt so in control. In the moment, no question, but in control and able to do what I pleased, when I pleased, how I pleased, in my efforts to please her.

My hand found a way to leave her breasts and move to the lock in the door, where I found the keys inserted but abandoned. I turned the key, and the pressure of our bodies caused the door to explode open and we tumbled inside, falling to the floor as one. Never ceasing kissing, we rose and moved to the staircase. We made it one carpeted step before Melissa fell backwards and I on top of her. Thinking outside myself I ripped open Melissa's blouse as her hands moved to my belt. My mouth shot to the small space between her perfectly round breasts as I felt Melissa's hand slide inside my pants. Good God how could she make me harder than I was? And yet she did.

My mouth explored, independently, while my hands moved to my own hips as I struggled to slide my pants down with no disruption to anything already in motion. We ambled up two more steps which, if nothing else, helped me to shed my pants and change my focus to Melissa's. Those came off much more easily and I honestly cannot recall if her panties came off with them, or she was not wearing any to begin with. Bottom line: nothing was between us now.

As I was already on top of Melissa I had just to move up one step and I was instantly and deep inside her. She let out a howl of a gasp as her head arched backward and her pelvis thrust upward to receive me. My hands now on the step for leverage, I drove deeper and she gasped deeper. She begged me to do what I was already doing, and had consumed my thoughts since that afternoon in the woods. I drove deeper, and faster, and Melissa's hips matched mine thrust for thrust. Her breathing intensified, and gasps heightened, louder, higher in pitch as I drove faster. Never too fast, but with an intensity we had not explored before. It was nothing I had ever experienced before.

In perfect unison our bodies worked, me feeling so at home inside her, filling her up as I swear I got even harder as I approached a now-inevitable climax. And I did. And she did. Melissa shuddered beneath me, me still very hard and remaining as deep as humanly possible. Suddenly she relaxed, and I collapsed on top of her. My mouth moved to hers and we kissed. A long, warm, and tender kiss. Melissa looked at me, and spoke.

"What's your name again?"

"Dirk," I replied. "Dirk Golddust."

"That your porno name?"

"What do you think?"

"I like it. Suits you."

"I'm glad you approve."

"You okay?" she asked.

"What do *you* think?"

"You seem okay."

"I'm okay." I smiled as I peered down at her exquisite face and moved a strand of hair

140

away from her eyes. "More than okay."

"Me too," Melissa added.

***

Butt naked, we lay on a rug beneath a thin blanket in the den. Adding to the sheer romance, the Golf Channel was on the big screen in the background. And I mean *big* screen. Spooning, and chatting, audio from the television caught our attention.

"This week marks not one but two inaugural events. The Husky Open debuts on the Canadian Tour, in Heaven, British Columbia, while on the big tour the Seattle Classic takes center stage. While many of the Tour's stars are taking this week off after last week's major, Andy Jones will be teeing it up in the Emerald City, much to the delight of Pacific Northwest residents."

Neither of us said a word, at first, until Melissa quipped, "Big tour".

"Well, it is," I affirmed. After a pause, I added, "They mentioned Andy; did they mention me? If they did I didn't catch it." Melissa burst a laugh.

"You know, I don't think they did mention you. That is quite an omission. I know some people at the Golf Channel, I may write a letter."

"Two e's in Green," I reminded her.

"Green? But you said your name was Golddust. Cad."

John Westley

Chapter ~~69~~ 17

If it is not obvious by now, I did have a nice, late tee time for round one. Noon; my favorite tee time. When people talk about whether they are morning or night people, I am quick to point out I am a noon person. For one, it is lunch time and who does not like lunch? You can sleep in and still make noon appointments (if you cannot make a noon appointment on time, you have bigger issues). It is never, ever, dark at noon. You can drink at noon. You can pretty much do anything you want to… at noon.

I bogeyed the first hole. Okay, that is not a great testament to the whole loving noon thing, but I never said noon was perfect. What was perfect was the weather, the conditions, my caddy; too many things to let a bogey bother me. I backed up that contention by rebounding with par, birdie, birdie on the next three holes to get me to one under, which is where I stayed until the fourteenth hole. Another set of back-to-back birdies followed by three safe pars and I was in at three under, and three back of the lead.

"It's my fault you shot 69," Melissa declared.

"How so?" I asked.

"I can't get that number out of my head. Tomorrow I will have to think of a lower number."

"I can live with 69," I said honestly. Four of them makes twelve under and wins the tournament, if you ask me. Just don't get it backwards."

That night we learned that Andy Jones shot 68 in Seattle. I do not know why it bothered me, it certainly should not have bothered me, but bother me it did. I know, I know, different course, different city, different everything. Hell, even a different par at 71. But he shot one lower than I did. I desperately tried not to (even internally in my own thoughts) debase what Melissa and I had going by saying to myself, *"Ya, but I'm shagging his wife"*. I really tried.

Chapter ~~69~~ 18

In the opening two rounds of a golf tournament one never gets two late tee times in a row. Typically a late tee time is followed up by an early one, and vice versa. That means *"Noon Person Green"* had a 7:08 tee time Friday morning. That also meant I was a good boy, Thursday night. I will not lie, it was thanks to Melissa I behaved. As I have noted more than once she really cared about me doing the best I could that particular week, and would have nothing to do with me getting tired before such an early start. We even slept in separate rooms. I know. Killed me. But she was also killing me with kindness – displaying such an obvious interest in my success that while I slept alone, it was with a warmth with which I was not heretofore familiar. And that warmth had nothing to do with the balmy, humid, summer air.

A 7:08 tee time at the height of the summer is an entirely different thing than a 7:08 tee time in early spring, or late fall. Especially in the Heaven, B.C. part of the world. The sun is up by 5:00 a.m., the air warm by 6:00 if it was ever cold, the light is perfect, nor is it too hot. In fact, you can be in by 11:00 and let the rest of the field swelter in the increasing heat, and play greens that are both drying out and speeding up.

Just listening to my open-minded optimism regarding an early tee time reminds me of a Gary Player story told by an old pro he often used to room with in the early days on Tour. Apparently one week Player returned to their hotel room and the pro asked him how the day went. Player replied that it was a great day; the greens were super fast, just how he liked them. Then I guess it was a week or two later, and a similar scenario: Player returned to the room and as a matter of course the pro asked him how his round went? Player said it was a good day, the greens were soft and slow and he liked them that way. The old pro expressed confusion, telling Player *"one week you like the greens fast, the next week you like the greens slow. What gives?"* Player just looked at him and said,

"I don't know, I guess I just like whatever greens I'm lucky enough to play on."

Despite perfect conditions, and perhaps because I *am* Noon Person Green, I went twelve holes without a birdie. However, I also went twelve holes without a bogey. Then I played in birdie – par – birdie – par – birdie – par. Yup: 69. Six under, now tied for the lead but with no illusions, given I was one of the first groups off. There was *plenty* of time and plenty of players still on-course that could not just give that score a nudge, but leave it in their dust. The real question was would it be good enough to make the cut, which it most assuredly seemed it would be. It would have been quite remarkable if the cut line was at minus seven, especially given the scores from round one were, while low, average-low as opposed to super-low. The bottom line: it was reasonable to think I had easily made the cut, but bad luck to jump to that kind of assumption.

The next question was what to do? Hang around? Practice? Explore Heaven with Melissa? Come back to the club later to see what was going down? All of the above? We decided not to over-do anything. We had a bite to eat, nothing too much, then hit some balls. But not too many. A little bunker work, some chipping, some putting. All this and it was still only 2:00. But… easier to tell that minus six would make the cut with ample comfort. We went back to Melissa's, had a quick swim in her pool (nothing too strenuous and no, no hanky panky, not yet) and it was while we were getting changed afterward that we checked the internet to find I was as I had been 24 hours earlier. Three off the lead. I could not have been happier.

We switched on the television to see if the Husky Open would get any further mention on the Golf Channel, only to be greeted with the news that Andy Jones had inexplicably withdrawn from the Seattle Classic. He did not show for his tee time for round two, and that was all that seemed to be known. He had more or less disappeared.

"That's not like him, is it?"

"No, it's not," Melissa answered, feigning lack of concern but I could tell there was some.

"He's not likely to drink late, is he?"

"Oh, he could drink, and later than he ought to, but he never slept in a day in his life. And he would not have had a very early tee time," Melissa explained.

I mentioned earlier that for the first two rounds of a tournament, typically a player would get an early tee time followed by a late one, or vice versa, over Thursday and Friday. Of course, not every player can tee off first, or last. Therefore there are, for want of a better word, *medium* tee times, about mid-morning. So while the reverse of an early tee time is a late one, the reverse of a mid-morning tee time is… another mid-morning tee time. These are reserved for the veteran and star players who have paid their dues and earned a break from the early rise. Andy Jones was clearly a player who would, by default, be given a mid-morning tee time both Thursday and Friday, thus Melissa's assumption.

Speaking of tee times, the process changes for the weekend – rounds three and four. First of all, roughly half the field is eliminated (cut, thus the term *'the cut'*) from the tournament, and the remainder tee off Saturday in relation to their results. Leaders tee off last, so those furthest from the lead, but avoiding the cut, tee off first.

The order is changed again on Sunday for the exact same reason: leaders tee off last. It is actually a brilliant system that leads to heightened drama late Sunday afternoon, as your leaders come to the home stretch. It works not just for television, but for the on-course spectators too as they do not have to sprint all around the golf course to view the potential winners. Where I am going with this is that by virtue of my decent position heading into the weekend, I was given a later tee time for round three. This meant Melissa and I could go out for dinner and celebrate my making the cut. Which is exactly what we did.

Melissa took me to an Italian restaurant in town, not far from what I now called *my breakfast spot*. She promised that I would not be disappointed, and she kept her promise. I had been playing tournament golf for a fair time, and this was the first time my caddy ever bought me dinner. One bought me a hot dog lunch once, in Cincinnati (it was so remarkable I remembered the city, you see) but never dinner. Let alone at a posh Italian restaurant. Let alone wearing a short, form fitting, summer dress. Let alone in Heaven.

I did not notice until Melissa pointed it out that people were looking and commenting. Ah, life in a small town. Especially, I suppose, when your ex-husband is a famous local citizen. Not that I really had any idea how much time

Andy Jones ever spent in Heaven. He apparently owned two other homes, one on the east coast, in Florida, and another on the west coast, in California near Carmel. And, of course, he was on the road *a lot*. Melissa did say *'a lot'* with emphasis. One older lady stopped by our table and chatted briefly with Melissa, ignoring me completely, and left saying, "I hope Andy is okay." Now, that could have meant a hundred things. Most likely in relation to his pulling out of the Seattle Classic? Or was it something more sinister, as in poor Andy, his wife is moving on? Who knew? Did not really care. The lasagna was to die for. Little did I know.

The check came. Oh that was awkward. For me, not Melissa. She was sweet and nonchalant as she pulled out not a credit card but cash. It just felt bizarre for me to sit there and do nothing. Thank god she paid in cash (perhaps, knowing Melissa, she did this on purpose) and we did not have to sit and wait for the server to bring back the slip for her to sign. I guess it felt awkward because it happened so rarely. I once had a boss who said the key to fighting over the check is to *'reach fast but fumble'*. He was known for avoiding paying. The women I had associated with never even reached, let alone fumble. And I am just talking about the ones who *invited me* to dinner. And chose the restaurant. And ate well. It would actually become funny (to me) when the bill *did* arrive and I would just let it sit there for a while. To see if they would even glance at it. Of course, they never did. Though one must have as they commented on the inadequacy of the tip I left.

The awkward bill-paying out of the way, we walked out the restaurant door to a brilliant summer evening. We had parked across the road and a split second after we stepped forward onto the street a pick-up truck came out of nowhere, speeding, and nearly ran us down. I grabbed Melissa and threw her back onto the sidewalk, me tumbling after her. I can joke now that it was akin to Wile E. Coyote being run over by a bus on an empty desert highway, but at the time it was not funny at all. It was that close. Poor Melissa was a bit banged up having been thrown to the concrete. I could not feel bad about that, however, given what the alternative might have looked like.

What must have been funny would have been to watch us attempt to cross the street again. Quiet as before, each of us taking one single step forward, as if testing the temperature of the water at a pool. Then, once into the street, hurrying - not so much as to look ridiculous, but enough to avoid a possible repeat scenario. This time we agreed I would drive as Melissa was clearly still a little shaken up. I will not lie, after the slight emasculation of the check-paying, it was nice to play hero *and* to drive her Beemer.

***

The night was still young, and it was also still light out when we arrived back at Melissa's. That time of year it remains light until 10:30, so a swim seemed in order. Melissa disappeared and returned in a stunning white bikini. I had my one pair of board shorts that got plenty of use. Worse, they were not very supportive. Not generally a problem except when you are hanging around a woman that makes Bo Derek look plain. If you get my drift. We swum just a few minutes and then retired to deck chairs which I had positioned to catch the last few rays of warm evening sun. The sun was exhilarating, but once it too retired the air was still very warm and comfortable as we lay on the chairs, side-by-side, holding hands. My left hand holding her right, my right hand holding a local *Kokanee* beer, her left hand holding a cider of some sort. Heaven.

Heaven was disturbed. By a very loud *crack* ringing out through the night air. I heard it as I was walking out front to my car in search of a Camille Miller CD I wanted Melissa to hear. Me in my swimsuit and a t-shirt, I looked up to see it must have been a backfire from yet another pick-up truck as it sped by the house on this usually quiet suburban street. Melissa ran out the front door, if not concerned clearly curious about what had caused such a noise.

"Just a backfire, a pickup truck going by."

"God, I thought it was a gunshot," Melissa declared. "Did you see this pickup truck?

"Ya, an older brown one. Something about Wood Brothers on the back I thought. But I'm not sure."

"Wood Brothers?" Melissa seemed shocked.

"I don't know, it could have said Woolly Mammoth for all I know it was going quite fast." Melissa stared out and down the street, as if to see the truck that had long since departed.

"What?" I asked.

"It's just that the truck that nearly hit us after dinner…"

"Yes?"

"I could have sworn that was a Wood Brothers truck."

"But that truck was blue," I pointed out. This one was definitely brown."

"They're brothers. Tommy and Brian Wood. One has a blue truck; the other has a brown one."

"Oh," I said, trying to register. "It is a small town," I added.

"It is," Melissa conceded, "But one truck nearly hits us in town, and the other shows up on my street which is half way up the mountain?"

"Maybe one of them lives around here?" I tried.

"No, they both live in the poor part of town. Sorry, that sounds bad, but it's true."

"They're in construction, correct?"

"Yes," Melissa answered.

"Maybe he was checking on a site up here?"

"That could be true, I never thought of that," Melissa confessed. I really was not sure what she was fussed about, but glad she was beginning to settle down. I had found the Camille disc I wanted to play for her and convinced her to come inside to have a listen.

Chapter ~~69~~ 19

We skipped breakfast out and got to the golf course in plenty of time for my 11:52 tee time. It did not take being at the club long to realize something was up. There was a buzz beyond the fact that it was the weekend, and we soon found out why. PGA Tour star Andy Jones was in the house. Did not see that one coming.

Nor did I physically see Jones until I strode to the first tee around a quarter to noon. My time. Prior to that, with Melissa at my side, I went about my normal prep routine for a tournament round of golf. There was much talk about Andy Jones being on-site, and about a half dozen theories as to why he had pulled out of the Seattle Classic a day earlier, and was in Heaven that day. But nothing concrete. He obviously was not too ill, if at all, as he had been made Honorary Starter for the day. The starter is the person responsible for making sure the players tee off on time, and in the right order. When the Three I's are not playing, of course. An Honorary Starter just shadows the starter, meets and greets, playing a token role as the title might imply.

As I hit the tee box the starter introduced me to Jones, who smiled broadly and extended his hand, saying, "I'm Andy Jones."

"Mr. Jones, this is Dan Green, from Oregon," the starter explained.

69 Shades of Green: 7 Days in Heaven

"Pleasure to meet you, Mr. Jones," I said, somewhat sincerely.

"I've heard a lot of good things about you, Don," Jones said. This had to be a lie. In my mind I was full of promise, but had no illusions about being 'known' in the golf world. The only people who knew me were guys I had had a beer with on the circuit, and many of them had forgotten me afterward. That said, I had no doubt that he knew who I was, and had heard 'things' about me. He still had not let go of my hand. "Play well," he added, giving my hand an extra firm squeeze before moving on to the other player in my group who had arrived right behind me.

I will not lie, I was nervous as hell teeing off. I had been under much greater pressure – theoretically – before. I felt more *watched* this day. A re-affirmation of my solid golf swing lay in the fact that, despite my nerves, I ripped a drive down the right side, and this time it did draw back to the middle, rolling a little left of center. The gallery at the tee – larger than usual because of the presence of star Jones – applauded warmly which buoyed my ego greatly.

What about Melissa you are wondering? Good question. She hung out by my bag, said not a word, and had absolutely no interaction with Andy. Until we walked off the tee toward the first fairway, at which time Andy said,

"Hello, Melissa."

"Hello," came the reply, with a small polite smile, but without slowing as she lugged my tour bag in pursuit of my perfect drive.

***

My good play in the first couple of rounds had two likely directions it could go: better, or worse. On this day, it got better. Far better. Birdied one, three, five, seven and eight to hit eleven under for the tournament and, at that point, a one-shot lead. Aside from my obvious confidence in my swing, it seemed all the stimulation swarming around me was doing me good. My life was suddenly surreal, why not my golf game too? This thought allowed me to not doubt what was going on, and just flow with it. And flow I did. Three more birdies and oops, one bogey on the back nine for a day's total of 65. And you thought I was going to shoot another 69.

I might have been thrown off had I known Andy Jones followed me for a couple of holes. I say me, he was no doubt following Melissa. Nonetheless I was glad my focus was such that I did not know, and Melissa herself certainly never let on. It was still a mystery what had caused Andy to withdraw from the Seattle event. He appeared to be perfectly healthy.

I, on the other hand, while mentally delighted, was feeling my back again. Just a teeny bit. Not enough to worry about, but just enough to worry about. I hesitated mentioning it to Melissa for fear she might think I was just after another massage.

"My back is bothering me a tiny bit," I said. Okay, so I did not hesitate for very long.

"Well, we know what to do," she quickly replied. I smiled, and was instantly reminded of a story involving my college roommate. His car would not start and he came back into the apartment we were sharing, walked right past me, picked up the phone and called his father. I need to point out that his father lived a good hour away. Toward the end of the phone conversation I could hear my roommate stressing, "No, dad, I don't want you to. No! Don't bother, I'll solve it!" He then hung up in a temper, and I asked what the matter was? He answered, "It's my dad; he's going to drive all the way out here to look at my car, even though I told him not to!"

"Why the hell did you phone him then?" I exclaimed with a laugh. "You knew darned well he was going to jump in his car to come fix yours, that's why you called him!" He knew I was right. The moral of this story? I was about to get another massage.

***

John Westley

Melissa sent me to the *'massage room'* the moment we arrived home. She instructed me to remove my shirt and lie down while she went to change out of her sweaty caddying clothes. She returned in short shorts and the tightest t-shirt I had seen her wear yet. I wondered to myself how she even got it over her head, when I should have been wondering about how I was going to get it back over her head! Melissa put on some music and dimmed the lights, to set a relaxing mood. You know.

Surprisingly, or perhaps not surprisingly at all, we had yet to talk about Andy's presence at the golf course that day. Until then.

"So that was a bit of a surprise, seeing Andy at the golf course. I'm not sure if it threw you or me more. Seemingly me!" I said.

"Well, if shooting 65 is throwing you..." she replied.

"That was bizarre." There was a pause, in talking only, as her strong hands dug into my shoulder muscles. "He was shorter than I expected," I added. Melissa laughed and as she continued to massage I could feel her lean in, and her breasts touch my back. Incredible. "And uglier," I said, wondering what kind of reaction that might get. Her breasts pushed more firmly into my back. I smiled. "And was that a bit of a speech impediment?" I asked incorrigibly. Melissa climbed up onto the massage table, straddled my hips, and continued to work my shoulders. Her hands then moved down my back, occasionally working gently, occasionally with great strength. She leaned forward and moved her mouth toward my ear,

"Roll over," she whispered.

With great balance she stood, and I rolled over as requested. Melissa lowered herself down onto me, still straddling, her breasts ready to burst from her oh-so-tight shirt. She leaned forward and pressed her lips to my neck, then my cheek, then my ear, and finally my own lips. I was happy with any or all of the above. The mood was perfect, until the lights went out. I realized too, the music had stopped. The power was out. Melissa sat up.

"That's odd," she said.

"Power outage?"

"Guess so. We get them a lot in the winter, but never in the summer."

"Where is the fuse box? Want me to go look?" I asked.

"Would you? It's just in the furnace room down the end of the hall."

Melissa got down from the massage table and moved to an end table with an unlit candle on it. She was reaching for a lighter as I left the room. I began to make my way down the hallway when I heard a noise from the floor above. I stopped. Listened. It was not my imagination, as I heard a noise again. I turned and headed instead toward the stairs. It was a wide but not very high, yet curved set of stairs. I climbed them quietly, still listening. I heard a noise again, coming from the direction of what I called the golf museum. Andy Jones' den.

Curtained French doors led to the den, and one was ajar. I pushed it open and entered, slowly. Perhaps too slowly, or not slowly enough, as the next thing I knew I was flat on my face on the ground, my head ringing. I looked up and saw both who and what hit me. I rolled out of the way before a golf club swung down at me furiously. It seemed my assailant understood the principle of hitting down. A gruff looking, unshaven man, perhaps in his thirties or even forties, although I did not have time to make notes for the sketch artist as the intruder raised the club once more. I yanked on the rug and while not as swift as in the movies, it was enough to cause him to lose his balance and abort his next attempt to drive me into oblivion. I rolled again and tackled his legs, bringing him down on top of me.

I grappled with him for what seemed minutes but may have been a fraction thereof. I managed to get out from under him – he was much heavier than I would have imagined – and quickly got two shots in. Two furious blows with my right, surprising him I am sure, but more so myself as I had not been in a fight since my high school days. Before that, even. Hell, I am a golfer, not a fighter. I say surprised him, but it sure did not finish him. Angered him, more like. He threw me off of him, but fortunately toward a bag of golf clubs. While this gave me the opportunity to arm myself to match my combatant, I instantly realized the clubs I was reaching for were antiques. And worth who knows how much. Stupid, I know, but I chose the clubs over me and looked for another option.

Wham! His club-weapon just missed me and took out an expensive looking lamp. Hell, everything in that room looked expensive. I leapt over the back of the couch to temporary safety as he chased me round. He took another swing at me, and missed again. He was clearly coming over the top, but I was not of the mindset to help him with his swing just then. I suddenly remembered that I had left my golf clubs inside the front door, and made a mad dash to exit the den. I got to them quickly enough, but unfortunately my excellent caddy had been too diligent in buttoning and zipping up the bag's hood. I fumbled as my assailant approached. I reached, I grabbed, I pulled, and swung, hitting him right in the mid-section and ruining a perfectly good umbrella at the same time. This bought me enough time, though, to get into the bag and retrieve my one-iron. Yes, I carried a one-iron.

With apologies to my Tofino golf coach, I skipped my pre-shot routine and swung. I was not yet willing to go for his head and knew if my shot was ill-placed the club would just break over his arm. The clubhead struck his forearm perfectly, causing him to yell *and* drop the club he was wielding. I swung again and got the other arm. I was lying two and had to make my third shot count. I caught him in the chest which sent him reeling backward toward the staircase, but my club broke in the process. *Shit!* I ran forward and tackled him, sending him, and me, down the stairs. I wound up on top and while he may already have been out, I threw a wild roundhouse punch to ensure he was down for good. That was when I heard it, and my heart almost stopped.

Her screams were blood curdling. Coming from the massage room. I ran to the door and could see the massage table had been knocked over, and I could see the back of a man, the same size or bigger than the one I had just fought with, on his knees. I shot forward and could see Melissa beneath him, struggling for dear life. Gripping the broken end, I swung the handle end of my golf club, this time not hesitating to go for the head. It was over that quickly. He fell to one side, and Melissa pulled herself out from beneath him and ran to me, hugging me, clinging to me for dear life.

Chapter ~~69~~ 20

"Are you okay?" I asked, very concerned as I had no idea what had happened to her before I arrived. Melissa did not answer me, she just kept clinging.

"Those bastards. I had a bad feeling," she finally said.

"Wood brothers?"

"That's Tommy," she said pointing down at the ground. "I heard you fighting and came out, and he grabbed me. Are *you* okay? What happened?

"I heard someone in the den, I went in to look and the other one, I guess that was…"

"Brian."

"He sucker punched me."

"Are you okay? Where is *he?*"

"I think I'm okay; he's lying at the bottom of the stairs right now. We should call the police."

"My phone's upstairs."

I took Melissa by the arm and led her out of the massage room and toward the stairs. I stopped us cold in our tracks. The one I left at the bottom, Brian, was nowhere to be seen. Gone.

"Shit," I said. "He's gone."

"Oh my god," Melissa gasped with terror, "We have to get out of the house."

I tightened my grip on her and we raced up the steps. The front door, to our right, was wide open. Rather than risk another sucker punch, we simply burst out the front door and across the lawn to my Corolla parked on the street. No way were we going into the garage for her Beemer, as nice a ride as it is. We got to my car and heard a noise coming from the front door. It was Tommy, standing there like an ape, with blood dripping down the side of his head. He yelled something indeterminable as I shoved my hand in my pocket for my keys. Which were not there, as I had removed them prior to lying down on the massage table.

"No keys?" Melissa screamed in a panic.

"Hang on," I said, as I dropped to the ground. Tommy started to move toward us. I reached under the car and much to my relief was able to quickly feel and find a key magnet box I had stuck there, for just such an occasion. You know, for when a bloody, big gorilla of a guy is trying to kill you. I unlocked the front passenger door and dived in. I was all for ladies first, typically, but knew I had to get to the driver's side and Melissa could jump in after me, which she did, quickly pulling the door closed behind her.

I cannot pretend Tommy was moving quickly, but he was moving steadfastly in our direction. I saw no reason to stick around and see what he wanted, so I started the car. If this was the movies the car would have had trouble starting, but this was a Corolla and it fired up quickly and I pulled away even quicker. So quick in fact, that it was not long before we caught up with the other Wood brother's pick-up truck. Not my intention! Melissa screamed, and I hair-pinned a right down a neighboring street. Not sure how I did not hit anything as I drove with my eye fixed on the rear view mirror to see if he was in pursuit. It seemed he was not, and with Melissa's guidance we drove straight to the local Royal Canadian Mounted Police station.

***

Despite all the drama, I got a weird kick out of the fact that we were going to the Mounties. I had grown up on re-runs of Dudley Do-Right cartoons, replete with Rocky and Bullwinkle, so it seemed a little surreal that suddenly I was in need of cops who get their man. In this case, brothers. My first disappointment was that none of the cops we saw were wearing the famous red uniform of the Mounted Police. Apparently that is ceremonial dress, and on the job the Canadian Mounties dress pretty much as any police unit does. Remarkable was the fact each and every one of them wears a bullet proof vest. On any other day I would have wondered, in a peaceful small town like Heaven, whether there was a high incidence of hunters' bullets ricocheting off moose? But on this day the quaint little country town seemed a little less safe, and Kevlar vests more warranted.

I referred to the Mounties' headquarters as a police station, but truthfully it was more akin to a bungalow. There were two officers on duty, and through dumb luck a local paramedic was visiting for coffee. I say dumb luck, because it was several minutes before anyone, myself included, noticed that I was standing in a pool of blood. My left arm was bleeding. This was not good. Not for a professional golfer. Not for a professional golfer who was playing well, and in contention at a tournament. The paramedic immediately wrapped my arm to stop the bleeding and took me into another room for closer examination. It seems, whether by a knife I never saw, or more likely from the broken shaft of the golf club I was wielding, my arm had been sliced. Golfers do not like slices, remember.

There was obvious confusion among the three – cops and paramedic – in terms of prioritizing taking my statement or getting me to the hospital for stitches. In the end it was decided one officer would accompany me in the ambulance to take my statement on the way to the Emergency Room, while Melissa remained and continued to give her statement at R.C.M.P. Headquarters.

If you were wondering whether I was concerned about my left arm and my ability to play the next day, I cannot say it did not enter my mind. I can say the fact someone had just tried to kill me was beginning to settle at the forefront of my thoughts to a greater degree. My initial reaction was one of relief; that it was my left arm and not my right. One of the keys to my improved game was understanding that your naturally dominant arm should be your dominant arm when hitting down at the golf ball as well. For years I had struggled – with no sound reasoning – to swing the club with my weaker, less coordinated left arm while trying to get my right arm to quiet down. The old-school saying was *let the right arm go along for the ride.* This change in understanding led to an instant improvement in my downswing, with the only obstacle being my years of training my arms to do it the wrong way. It turns out, however, it is much easier to re-program a dominant arm to be dominant again, than the other way around. So, ever one to look for a silver lining, I quickly rationalized that a hurt left arm would submit more and allow the more powerful right arm do its job.

Eleven stitches later and Melissa arrived at the hospital to pick me up. The doctor told me to *'take it easy'* on my arm, and I made zero mention of the fact I was, in theory, to play one of the biggest golf rounds of my life on Sunday.

John Westley

Needless to say I was glad to see Melissa, and it is funny to say now but she brought me a present. As a result of initiating my massage I had gone through this entire ordeal... shirtless. The hospital had loaned me a standard issue gown, but Melissa arrived with an official, souvenir, Canadian Mounties' t-shirt. Which she had to pay for; apparently you do not get a free one per visit.

The next question was what to do next. I had jumped to the conclusion it would not be safe to go back to Melissa's house, and I already knew all the hotels and motels in town were booked up. However, Melissa's house was *the* safest place to go as the police were already there beginning their investigation. This was no routine house burglary, therefore forensic investigators were being sent for from a neighboring, bigger, town. In the meantime the local Mounties were there securing the crime scene and would remain all night until the out-of-town investigators arrived. So to Melissa's home we went.

It was disturbing to Melissa to return to her home which was now labeled a crime scene. Yellow police tape already roped off sections of the front, blood was evident on the floor, broken glass was strewn everywhere; it was all a little surreal. And I am honest when I say that all the evening's events were a little bigger than my golf tournament. I was not even sure if I would play - I was more worried about Melissa. The one thing I knew was I was not teeing off until 1:00 p.m. so at the very least I was not worried about an early tee time if I did decide to play.

As one officer roamed around the house taking photographs, Melissa and I finally had a chance to sit and talk about what had transpired. What was obvious was that the Wood brothers were after us. And that Melissa's seeming paranoia about one brother almost hitting us with his truck, and the other brother *'backfiring'* on her street (presumably now a gun shot had been fired) had not been paranoiac at all. We knew for sure who was after us, but had no idea why. Apparently, at the R.C.M.P. headquarters, Melissa had been questioned thoroughly about any possible relationship between the Wood brothers and, of all people, her ex-husband Andy Jones. And there was a relationship. Andy had once hired the Woods to build a spec home that they would later try to flip, and there was some question about someone owing someone that evil word: money. The plot thickened. We debated theories, now over a much-needed bottle of scotch, as to what might be going on. What became evident was Melissa expected me to play the next day, and she was going to be on my bag.

Chapter ~~69~~ 21

It was an odd sleep Saturday night. There was no thought of sleeping separately for the sake of my game; Melissa clung to me the entire night, head on my chest, leg draped over mine, one hand clinging to my shoulder. The trick was giving my left arm some space so as not to disturb the fresh stitches.

The issue of whether to play or not was settled by the Mounties. They wanted us out of the house so their team of crack forensic investigators could work on getting their man. The fact it was Sunday had no bearing on them getting started early, so we departed the house much sooner than I needed to prepare for the day's round. It was clear Melissa had seen enough of my Corolla so we climbed into the Beemer and decided to attempt, at least, to cheer ourselves up and return to some sense of normalcy - bearing in mind we had only known each other a week - by visiting my favorite breakfast place in downtown Heaven.

We began the trek down the mountain by noting, aloud, that at least the weather was remaining fantastic. Funny how sunshine *can* improve even the gloomiest of days. Our conversation quickly switched, however, from the barometric pressure to hypothesizing about our recent, quite dramatic, turn of events. We had been assuming that the Wood brothers were after us. And as I was nobody to them, we had narrowed that down to Melissa. But coincidental with recent activities was Andy Jones' hasty departure from Seattle, and surprise return to Heaven. What if someone was in fact not trying to kill us, but kill Andy and we were just in the wrong place at the wrong time? Okay, times?

"Someone *is* trying to kill me," Andy said as his head popped up from the back seat. Melissa screamed and the car swerved dramatically.

"Andy! What the hell are you doing back there?" Melissa asked after recovering control of the car (thank god) and staring into the rear view mirror – a little too long for my comfort.

"Someone is trying to kill me," Andy repeated. "They followed me to the house and I hid in your car."

"But it was locked!"

"I have a key, Melissa."

"Why didn't you drive away then?"

"I couldn't get out of the garage, you changed the code. Why did you change the code?"

"Never mind why I changed the code, what is going on? Do you realize we were almost killed last night?"

"Cry me a river, so was I!"

"It's always about you, isn't it Andy? Poor you, you were nearly killed, never mind how many bodies you leave in your wake."

"It's Don, isn't it?" Andy said addressing me, and even extended his arm over the seat to shake my hand. Oddly hospitable.

"Hi," I said in response, not really knowing what else to say. Not even to correct him on my name. As we approached a stop street Melissa again panicked,

"Oh no!"

"What?" I asked.

"My brakes. They're not working!" She pumped the brakes feverishly but there was little response as we approached the intersection. "Is there anyone coming?"

I looked left and right and left again, "No, coast is clear!" We sailed through the intersection, speed building, and the tension continued to build as well when Andy then called out,

"Shit!"

"What?" I asked, turning back toward him and then seeing the same thing he did. A Wood Brothers construction pick-up came hurtling over the crest of the hill into sight, in hot pursuit. I was quite sure it was not to rescue us from our brakeless plight.

"Speed up!" Andy screamed, and not in a very masculine manner.

"Speed up? What goddamned choice do I have? I can't slow down!" Melissa cried in response, quite accurately.

"Gear down," I cried, but in a determinedly more calm manner.

"What do you mean?"

"Your gears, shift to third!" Melissa responded admirably but our speed was still mounting and, despite it, the pick-up truck was gaining on us.

Not that we needed a push, but a shove is what we got as the pick-up rammed us from behind. To make sure we knew they were there, it rammed again. Another intersection was approaching and again the same cry to see if anyone was coming. One car was.

"Car, to your right!" That car reached the four-way before us, which of course under normal circumstances gave it the right to move through the intersection first. Astutely Melissa leaned on, and did not back off of the horn. She let it blast, and you could see the car to our right stutter start. That is, it began to move but immediately stopped. Good for them; they would live to see another day as we, and the pick-up on our tail, sped through and continued down the mountain road.

Down was where we were headed, and things were not looking up. Not, that is, until we heard the sweet sweet music of the Mounties' sirens. A quick look back revealed not one but two cop cars in pursuit. I quickly imagined Nelson Eddy driving one patrol car and Brendan Fraser the other. They managed to book-end the pick-up and force it to the shoulder of the road. Once the Wood truck was brought to a halt the inner of the two R.C.M.P. vehicles continued on, in pursuit of us.

"Gear down again," I yelled to Melissa. "Second, shift to second!" She did and the transmission screamed, while the car jolted not to a stop, by any stretch, but to a quasi-reduced speed at least. Of all things, the car's phone suddenly rang. The call display showed "RCMP".

"Hello?" Melissa answered in a stressed tone.

"This is the police, pull your vehicle over. I repeat, pull over."

"I can't! No brakes!"

"No brakes!" Andy and I repeated the phrase in eerie unison.

Alertly the R.C.M.P. squad car powerfully moved ahead of us and pulled in front.

"What is he doing?" Melissa cried.

I almost laughed, "They're going to slow us down!"

Indeed, the police car slowed brilliantly, and allowed us to love tap it in the rear. Then again, but allowing us to lean on their back bumper. Smoke from the police car's brakes blinded us as they continued to reduce their speed. The Beemer made contact intermittently until such time as we were literally impressed upon their back bumper.

"Follow me, regardless of where I go," came the authoritative voice over the phone. Melissa obeyed and, still pressed against the squad car's back bumper, she steered with it as it turned into a field where there was no ditch between it and the country road. Slower, slower, slower as both cars were further slowed by the long grass of the field. Finally, stopped. Despite being quite shaken up the three of us cheered much the same way a plane full of North American air travelers might once hitting the runway after a trip to an undesirable country. We were stopped, and alive, thanks to the Mounties. Oh Canada.

The cheering did not last long. The police officer was barely out of his car for us to thank when we heard an ominous sound. Not for a moment did we think it was a backfire, even though it came from the exact location of the pick-up truck that had befuddled us just a day earlier. Two loud shots rang out. Our hero Mountie ran to the road and looked back up the hill. He paused and then ran back to his own vehicle in time to hear, over his radio,

"Shots fired. Officer down."

We were left standing, understandably enough, as he leapt back into his car, fired it up and yanked on the steering wheel to return to the road. He sped up the hill with lights and sirens on all cylinders.

John Westley

***

There was good news and bad news. And good news… and bad news. The first set of good news was that, despite the fact the other officer was hit, due to the Mounties' policy of wearing Kevlar he was not badly hurt and would survive with bruises. The bad news was that the driver of the pick-up truck, who was apparently Tommy Wood, got away. By the time our hero officer arrived the other officer was down and out, and Wood was nowhere to be seen. A fugitive, on the loose.

The second bit of good news was I was given the Mounties' permission to go play my final round, with their blessing and good luck. They were more preoccupied, again understandably, with getting their injured officer to hospital. The second set of bad news, though? Guess where my golf clubs were? Oh, I had not forgotten them; not at all. But I had put them, naturally enough, in the trunk of the car. The trunk of the car… that had just been rammed repeatedly by a speeding pick up truck. My eight and nine irons survived. As for the rest; well let's just say it was not a pretty picture.

"Oh, that's not good," Andy pointed out as we opened the trunk.

"I've seen worse," I joked as I looked at my poor clubs.

"You have?" Melissa asked sincerely.

"Not really," I confessed. Bizarrely – or so I thought – Andy came and stood right next to me. That *in your personal space* kind of stance.

"You know, we are about the same height," Andy stated.

"Yes," I agreed, not quite cluing in why my new girlfriend's old husband was sizing up his old wife's new boyfriend. If I could be so bold as to declare myself that.

"Hold out your arm," Andy directed, adding to the bizarreness. Just as bizarre, I did not question and did as he asked. He then stood shoulder to shoulder with me and extended his arm alongside mine. "Pretty similar," he added.

"Okay," I said.

"You can use my clubs. They're at the club." That was when the penny dropped and I felt a bit of a dolt for not catching on sooner. To be fair, it had been a hectic couple of days.

"Use your clubs?" I asked, incredulously.

"Use *your* clubs?" Melissa asked, equally mystified.

"Sure, why not?"

"Um, because you never let anyone touch your clubs," Melissa replied. "Not even me."

"Well that's different," Andy said. You could see that got Melissa's ire up.

"How on earth is that different?" Melissa demanded to know but I jumped in before the gloves came off and interrupted with,

"I would love to borrow your golf clubs. If you're sure you don't mind."

"It's rather exceptional circumstances," Andy declared accurately, "and I do feel somewhat responsible so by all means, my clubs are your clubs. If you win today you can buy me a beer."

"I'll buy you a beer regardless," I stated with glee.

"Wait a minute!" Melissa shouted out. "Can we end the male love-in and get to the golf course?"

"Certainly," I said.

"Do you want to come with us?" she asked Andy.

"No, I want to stand in the middle of this corn field," he replied, "and thumb a ride."

Getting impatient Melissa continued with, "Well I'm just wondering because you're not making any progress toward getting in the car."

"Maybe I should drive," Andy added.

"*You* are not driving *my* Beemer!" Melissa boldly stated.

"*Your Beemer? Your Beemer?*"

I had the nerve to interject at this moment. "No one is driving this Beemer," I said. "Have you forgotten?"

"What?!" they both shouted at me, in perfect unison.

"The brakes. There are no brakes," I reminded everyone.

"Shit," they both swore. Again in unison. Ahhh, marriage. They made a cute ex-couple. And suddenly Andy's idea of thumbing a drive didn't sound that sarcastic after all.

***

It got worse.

"I can call Tori," Andy said in a solution-found kind of tone. I ducked.

"What?" Melissa screamed.

"She doesn't live far from here, she can come pick us up and get Don to the golf course in time to play."

"Dan," I offered.

"I'd rather walk," Melissa declared. I looked at her.

"But I don't have my phone; Melissa I need yours." Melissa just stared back at Andy, not moving a muscle. Without flinching Andy turned to me. "Don can I borrow your phone?" Who was I to argue? He did not fool around on me *and* he was just about to loan me clubs he won PGA events with. I handed Andy Jones my phone. Andy dialed.

"I see you have no difficulty remembering her number," Melissa quipped.

"Hello? Babe? Need your help. Bit of an emergency. Can you come pick us up and take us to the club? We're in that big field near the corner of Heavenview and a 101st. I'll explain when you get here. Us? Us is me, a pro named Don... Brown I think it is."

"Green."

"And..." Andy looked at Melissa as he hesitated. "And his caddy. Oh, and Babe, could you bring me a change of clothes? The ones I have on are past their due date. Thanks! See you soon."

"She has your clothes? Are you staying with her?"

"Well I had to stay somewhere; I didn't think I could stay with you and besides you have a houseguest in Don here."

"Dan."

"And why did you pull out of the Seattle tournament?"

"Oh, you knew about that?"

"I don't live in a bubble. It was all over the Golf Channel. Why did you withdraw?"

"I told you, someone is trying to kill me. Nobody knew where I was staying and yet I got a death threat at my hotel. Then Tori called my room and told me you were back and hanging out with some golf pro, who I now know to be Don here..."

"Dan."

"...who actually seems to be an okay guy, but anyway, I decided to get the hell out of there and I came straight here. That's about it," Andy explained. At the same time I made a decision not to bother trying to correct the Don thing.

Melissa looked perplexed. "No one knew where you were staying, yet you say Tori called you in your room?"

"Well, ya, I lost my phone, so I gave her the number there."

"And you have no idea who is trying to kill you or why?" Melissa asked.

"Clearly it is the Wood brothers, but I have no idea why. Tori and I invested in a house of theirs a while back, but I thought it went well."

"You don't owe them money?"

"No, I paid up front. If anything they owe me a couple bucks but it was not enough to even bother about."

"Wait a minute! *Tori* was your partner in this house?"

"Well ya, she is my dentist. I needed a write-off. She told me about this opportunity and it sounded good so I thought why not? What's wrong with that? If my dentist was a man and I invested in a house with him you wouldn't have had an issue."

"I would if you slept with him!" Melissa snapped back. I had to give that round to her.

By the time we got much further into another round the dentist in question showed up, honking. I grabbed my banged up golf bag as I still needed much of the contents, such as balls, gloves and so on, and we trudged our way through the long, dry grass to the edge of the road. Why we had not moved to the road sooner I am not sure. Because of the interesting conversation, I suppose.

Tori drove a huge, red Escalade SUV – just what every single female dentist needs. For transporting all that floss. I threw my bag in the back, Andy got into the front passenger seat, Melissa and I climbed into the back seat. Big, spacious, and comfortable, I have to admit, but I will never understand why *anyone* needs a vehicle that large. The whole way to the golf course Tori complained about the fact she was going to go to the club to watch the golf in the afternoon, and now she was having to make two trips. Which I calculated to be about six miles. But no questions about what had happened, were we okay (she said hello to me, ignoring Melissa completely) and why Melissa's car was now sitting in the middle of a farmer's field? I got a little sentimental, as her narcissistic behavior reminded me so of my ex-wife.

Chapter ~~69~~ 22

We arrived at the golf club and – superficially - nothing seemed any different than any other day during my seven days in Heaven. The majestic clubhouse persisted in basking in glorious sunlight, a slight breeze moved the leaves in the row of trees to one side of the, flags on the other. Oh, but what had transpired in those seven days! For a simple guy from Beaverton (Beaverton, Oregon) I had packed a lifetime of action into one simple Canadian week.

Despite all that had gone on that morning I was still in time to warm up "normally" for my round, given we had been kicked out of Melissa's house so early. And, despite all that had gone on that morning, *or because* of all that had gone on, I was very hungry. I am not sure if you are supposed to be hungry after repeated attempts on your life but I surely was, and knew I needed to get food in me before what was to be a big round of golf. With Andy Jones' clubs.

There was a buzz about the place as the final round of the tournament was under way. We went around to what is called the *'backshop'* - a very clever name for what is actually the *back* of the pro *shop*, where the members' golf clubs are stored. A young assistant greeted us with a smile, which broadened when he spotted Andy Jones.

"G'day, Mr. Jones," the assistant said with enthusiasm.

"Hey fella," Andy replied. "Can you pull out my clubs, I need to loan them to Mr. Green, here." A moral victory for me; Mr. Green was far more to my liking than *'Don'*. A moment later and the assistant, who was now obviously not that much bigger than Andy's staff bag, presented me with Andy's clubs. Andy pulled the irons and woods from the bag. My eye was searching for one thing: his putter. I was in extreme luck; we both used the same putter, an Odyssey tank. As a have-not mini-tour pro mine was an off-the-rack model, whereas Andy's had obviously been modified to his specifications but I was sure I could live with that.

"The rest is up to you now, my friend," Andy said warmly. As much as I wanted to dislike this guy – for the simple reason I was sleeping with his wronged ex-wife – I had to say I was impressed.

"Thank you," I said sincerely. "Now what will *you* do? As far as we know both the Wood brothers are still on the loose."

"For now, I am going to do something I rarely get to do."

"What's that?" I asked.

"Watch golf. This is probably the safest place I could be, at a golf course with thousands of spectators. No one is going to try anything here."

"Good point."

"After that, I'm not sure. With any luck the Mounties will have the Woods rounded up before the final putt drops. It will be hard for them to hide without going far from this town, and if they're far away I'm safe. For now at least." I shook Andy's hand and proceeded to the cafeteria to meet Melissa for a much desired meal.

***

Melissa had calmed down quite a bit by the time we sat down to some bacon and eggs. One of the things I loved about her was her sincere interest in seeing me do well, and she was already switching over to professional caddy mode. She had made a checklist for my pre-game warm up and was perusing the pages of our yardage book. I was guessing, too, that getting her head into my golf round was getting it out of the disturbing events of the morning. And by disturbing events, I think she was more annoyed with Andy's openness about Tori than the actual threats on all our lives.

On that note, while Melissa had switched into caddy mode, I myself had slipped into amateur sleuth mode. Andy had said someone was trying to kill him, which made it easy to forget that for the majority of attempts it had been Melissa and me who were on the receiving end. This was explainable, as the Woods could possibly have expected to find Andy and Melissa together, and I had simply been in the wrong place at the wrong time. Similar builds, both dressed like golf pros, a mix-up was feasible. But a common denominator was Melissa, and that worried me. She was either expendable collateral damage, or, possibly, the intended target. For now, though, the same theory applied to Melissa as Andy: nothing was likely to happen at a golf course crowded with thousands of spectators. With her on my bag, Melissa would be by my side all day and I would remain by hers afterward until we knew what was going on, and that she was safe. Beyond that, I had no idea what our future – that of Melissa and me – held.

There was less chatter between my caddy and me, which is natural both for a final round, and a day on which someone tried to kill you. My experience with the former, while not terribly extensive, was greater than with the latter. Thankfully. We hit balls, we chipped, we hit sand shots, we putted, and we grabbed a sandwich. The temperature was also climbing. By all accounts – namely the massive hand-painted leaderboard – no one was setting the course on fire, although with the heat a dropped cigarette might. The hot, dry conditions meant the greens would probably be lightning fast, and well trampled, before I hit even the first one.

And I was going to have to contend with a foreign putter. Familiar to some degree, yes, but nonetheless not identical to the one with which I had been playing so well of late. I decided, as I was wont to do in recent weeks, to look on the bright side and recognize that the sun was shining and I was contending in a golf tournament. Oh, and I was not dead.

What I have not mentioned yet is... I loved Andy Jones clubs. I loved his ex-wife, and I loved his golf clubs. You cannot get much deeper than that. If any negative thinking were to somehow permeate into my golf swing, my love affair with these golf clubs would surely erase that. The only unknown was yardages. I knew exactly how far *my* eight iron would send the ball, my seven iron, my five, and so on. While I loved how Andy's clubs felt, and the way the ball was flying, it was difficult in such a short time to get a handle on whether his eight iron sent the ball roughly the same distance as my eight iron did. This is a pretty significant factor in gauging exactly what club to use from a variety of distances, and a well-hit iron shot that sails five yards further than expected can mean, quite simply, a putt that is fifteen feet longer than it might have been. That in itself can be the difference between par and birdie, bogey and saved-par. There was no point obsessing about it though, I had to make do. Our goal, after long conference with my gorgeous caddy, was to proceed as if Andy's clubs were going to play the same as mine. If there was clearly a difference, and a trend in that difference, we would make allowances on the fly as the round progressed.

***

While only one shot back of the leader, I was in the second last group that Sunday and it suited me just fine. I was happy enough without the pressure of being in the very last group. Crazy as it might sound, I also preferred being one back as opposed to one ahead. I have always liked the underdog scenario (which I was, regardless) and the mental mindset is different when you feel the need to attack, rather than protect. It really should not be any different, especially in golf, yet it is.

My round started out rough. In the rough. My drive was not all that bad, but it was becoming apparent that Andy's driver shaft was a little stiffer than mine. While I have a tendency to leave shots a little right of center, this drive was right of right of center. Right rough. Consequently my approach shot came up just a little short, and to the right as well. I hit a great chip to six feet, but just lipped out the putt. Bogey. I did not panic; I was not upset with any of the swings I had made, things were just a little "off" and the result was a near-par. And yes, I realize a near-par is a bogey, but I could have saved par following some horrendous swings and been discouraged. I did not, and was not. I soldiered on.

A series of pars followed, and then another innocent bogey on the eighth to get to two over. I think at the time that had me four back, which could have been way worse if the leader, behind me, had gone on a tear.

I was walking up to the ninth tee when I saw Andy in the gallery. It looked like he had just arrived but I could not be sure. Silly as it sounds, I was just hoping he did not see my bogey the hole previous. Incredibly, as I stood on the tee waiting for the group ahead to hit their approach shots, Andy walked up onto the tee box – no marshal thought to stop him, he was Andy Jones after all – and stood beside me.

"How are the clubs?"

"Great," I said.

"You're fine. Don't panic. Just stick to your game plan." With that he gave me a pat on the shoulder and returned to the gallery. I was gobsmacked. Stick to your game plan. My Tofino guru had said the same thing repeatedly. Neither of them were the first to say that to a golfer, of course. But somehow it needed reaffirming at that moment, and it gave me a quiet confidence boost. I looked to the gallery, and there Andy stood, watching. I had not noticed before, and had no idea when she showed up, but Tori was there too. Standing next to Andy. It was all very strange. Seven days ago I had shown up in this beautiful small town, full of renewed optimism but knowing no one. Suddenly I felt like I had support. Granted it was odd support, in the form of an incredibly gorgeous and kind caddy, her adulterous ex-husband tour star, and his flaky, promiscuous dentist.

I cracked a drive.

I do not know how but this one turned over, moved from the right to the center, landed gently and rolled. I had 200 in on this par five, hit a three iron to six feet, and this time made the putt. Just like that I was even, two back of the leader, and back in it. Just like that, all hell broke loose.

***

I suddenly recognized someone in the gallery. It was one of the R.C.M.P. officers I had met the night of the first attack. As I glanced around I saw another officer I distinctly recognized, the hero from that morning. Were they here to watch me? Were they here *for* me? It seemed neither, as they were obviously searching the gallery. The drama built as suddenly there were at least six more Mounties in the gallery. All on the same side, to my left. They were looking for someone, and both

Melissa and I were standing in plain sight like sore thumbs, so it could not have been us.

Play ahead of us was continuing to be slow, and while that would have been annoying in another life right now it was fortuitous as it gave me the chance to observe what was going down in the gallery. That same morbid curiosity that takes us to smash-up derbies or causes us to slow and gawk as we pass by accidents on the freeway. I spotted Andy, who was clearly not aware of the police presence. That same presence was beginning to move toward him, however. Converge, in fact. All eight of the Mounties, and some others who I then realized were plain-clothes, moved in on Andy. They got to him, but it was Tori they surrounded. If anything, Andy was pushed out of the way. Suffice to say none of the cops asked for his autograph.

Others in the gallery either dispersed quickly, or conversely moved closer for a better look. There was much conversation - between the cops and a now irate Tori. Andy stood on the outside looking in, clearly not knowing what to do; not that there was much he could. One of the officers took Tori's arm and began to move it behind her back as another revealed handcuffs. Despite the army they had sent to apprehend her they obviously took her too lightly as she pulled her arm down and managed to escape them. Golf patrons all around, there was nowhere for her to easily go other than across the teeing ground, which she did. In a panic she sprinted up the tee box straight towards me. She was headed for a gap in the ropes behind me and the woods beyond. She either did not see me, or took me lightly, but she ran right by me. Without thinking I spun and dove, tackling her from behind and bringing her down to the ground as my fellow competitor also dove, but to get out of the way.

A second later a hockey team's worth of heavy-booted Mounties charged across the beautifully mown tee box, chewing up the grass as much as if they had indeed been mounted upon their steeds. This time they were far less polite as they yanked Tori's arms behind her back and cuffed her. They had got their man. I mean, dentist.

Chapter ~~69~~ 23

Melissa screamed and pointed. I immediately looked behind me as if Glenn Close had risen from the bathtub and was about to attack. Nothing. I then realized she was pointing at my arm. My left arm. Blood was pouring down it. I used to joke, to beginners, that if you see blood running down the shaft of your golf club you are gripping your club too tight. I knew in this instance I was either gripping my club too tight, or my stitches had ripped open.

My stitches had ripped open. Despite her panicked scream, Melissa leapt into action, grabbing a towel from my golf bag and rapping it tightly around my arm. A stream of people called for a medic who, due to my proximity to the clubhouse, was not long away. Not continuing was not an option in my mind. After all I had been through, and sitting within reach of the lead with a simple back nine to go, a little blood was not going to stop me. Okay, so it was a bit of blood. Some gauze, and some tape, and I was fine. In my mind. Blood always looks worse than it is.

I took some practice swings. I kept the most neutral look on my face I could muster, while deep down I can tell you now it hurt like hell. It was a different kind of pain; intense, but infinitely more bearable than say back pain. Back pain is debilitating, whereas this was just excruciating. I rationalized that the best solution was to swing within myself (what a concept) and to hit as few shots as possible (also a novel concept in golf).

I also had to hurry up. A blessing had been, and continued to be, the slow play of the group in front of us but now we had fallen behind them. I could tell the marshal was giving me some leeway but that would soon run out. Thanks to my eagle it was my honor so I rushed and pushed a tee shot down the tenth. I say pushed as it had little power, and it really was a push to the right rough. Deep rough was not what I needed with a damaged wing. I wedged out, and then hit a nice iron to ten feet from the pin, leaving me that distance for par. I struck a beautiful putt. And the short putt for bogey was technically perfect.

My back nine carried on in that vein, although not all were bogeys and I did even make a birdie. But my chances of winning slipped away like Mel Gibson's career. Seven pretty decent nines followed by one that was hemorrhaging, and there goes your ball game. The trick, as my beautiful caddy astutely pointed out to me (when not obsessing about my left arm) was to hang onto a spot in the top ten. A top ten finish would give me an exemption into the next event in Alberta in two weeks' time. This would give some time for my arm to heal, and there was no reason to think my decent play would go anywhere but east in that amount of time.

The good news was that, being in the second to last group, I knew exactly what I needed to shoot on the eighteenth hole to manage a top ten. Everyone but the two behind me had completed play, and it was pretty much a given that they would finish one-two. A birdie on the par five and I would be in a tie for tenth position.

A reachable par five, the only obstacle was a creek that crossed before the mouth of the green. I had one more excruciatingly painful drive to make, and it was an important one. Hell, they are all important. As the pain would be intense regardless, I decided to give it all I had. And it was a beauty. Not as long as when I was firing on all cylinders, but noticeably longer than my average for that nine. More importantly, it gave me a shot at reaching the green in two shots. A typical three iron stood between me and a putt for eagle, where birdie was required. Melissa put her hand on my shoulder. I looked down, and my left arm was bleeding again.

"It might be time to pack it in," she said.

"Get the gauze please," I asked in a calm voice. The medic had given us some extra – quite a bit of extra – gauze which Melissa had stowed away in my staff bag. To her credit, she did not argue nor did she waste any valuable time in returning with gauze and tape. She quickly wrapped some around my bleeding gam.

"My wedge," I said in a whispered voice – all I could manage at this point.

"What?"

"My pitching wedge." Melissa swiftly scooped my pitching wedge from the bag and handed it to me in return for my three iron. This was not going to be a sequel to Tin Cup. The pain in my left arm was now quite intense. Too intense. My mind flashed back to just two weeks earlier, in Tofino. My Canadian guru had me hit short irons with my right arm only, not for a few hours, but a few days. Several hours each day, for about four days. I took a few practice swings, holding the club with my right arm only. I closed my eyes and pictured Tofino: the peace, the rustic surroundings, and then the sound came alive. The sound of those surf waves crashing and hitting the beach. Each crash of a beautiful and natural wave coincided with my wedge making contact with the turf. With each practice swing I whispered to myself, *"hit down dammit!"*

I opened my eyes and addressed the ball. My right arm my only connection between me and Andy Jones' bloody pitching wedge. No more wasting time, I swung and hit a crisply perfect wedge to about one hundred yards out. With confidence that belied my energy level at that moment I marched downfield using the wedge as a walking stick. I was still away, as my playing partner was already dancing. Perfect, as this allowed me to walk straight up to my ball, set my club in the address position, and swing. Melissa later swore I hit that ball with my eyes closed. I find that hard to believe, but cannot say for sure. All I remember was the enormous cheer as the ball came to rest six inches from the beautiful round white cup on the eighteenth green.

My playing partner was an absolute gentleman as I arrived at the green and he said, "Play away; let me get the pin for you." Indeed, as Melissa walked my clubs to the back of the green he grabbed the pin for me, and using the same wedge that had not let me down the previous two shots I tapped in for a birdie. Safely in for T-10, as they say. And then I collapsed.

John Westley

Chapter ~~69~~ 24

I woke up in the medical tent. I have no idea how much time had elapsed but my first thought went to my scorecard. I knew I had to sign my scorecard, and that of my gentleman playing partner, Chris, for our scores to be official. I looked around and saw the loveliest vision. It was a bit surreal, being in a white tent on a sunny day. The cot I was on was white, there was a table and chair in the corner, both white. And there was Melissa, dressed in white, her tanned skin glowing. Insert died-and-gone-to-heaven joke here. I did not get a chance to open my mouth before Melissa handed me the two scorecards to sign. Love that girl.

I started to look at the scores, but realized things were not fully in focus.

"I checked everything, and so did Chris," Melissa explained.

"Double checked?"

"Double checked," she confirmed. I had no reason not to trust her. I scribbled my John Henry at the bottom of each card and Melissa immediately ran them out to the scorer's tent. Golf tournaments are all about tents, and trying not to get too tense. Go figure.

It is odd to say, but I missed her. Melissa. She had only run probably twenty yards away, and presumably would be back in a matter of moments, but it gave me such comfort to see her when I woke and I realized how much I needed her. Yes, needed. I am of the opposite view that you can want someone in your life, but you do not need anyone. I think we all need someone. The way we need food, water, and sleep. I was going to throw in cable TV but really do not want to distract from the fact that I mean what I say. We all *need* someone.

She returned. Thank god.

"What happened?" I asked.

"You finished tied tenth, just as we thought," she said with a sweet smile.

"No, what happened to *me?* I remember putting out, and then I am in here."

"You lost a bit of blood, is all."

"Oh, is that all?" She smiled again.

"You're okay. You lost some blood, got light headed, and fainted."

"I wish you had said *'collapsed'*. Fainted sounds so weak," I said, weakly.

"Okay, you collapsed in a dramatic heap on the eighteenth green," Melissa said melodramatically, followed by a sweet laugh.

"Oh my god, I just had the worst thought."

"What?" she asked, concerned.

"I didn't fall on Chris's line, did I?" Melissa laughed out loud.

"No, you were very conscientious in the way you fainted – I mean collapsed. I'm not kidding either, it really did look like you were trying to move away from his line. *And,* he made his putt, so it's all good."

"How did he finish, anyway? He was playing well."

"Sole second."

"Oh, that's great. I would have felt horrible if all the extracurricular antics had thrown him off. It wouldn't have been surprising."

"No, he's very happy, his first runner-up in a pro tourney he told me. He said he'd see you in Alberta for a practice round, if you want," Melissa said.

"Of course, that's nice; makes me feel better." I paused, trying to clear the cobwebs. I sat up and turned, putting my feet on the ground. That made me dizzy so I did not attempt to stand. "Tori," I said.

"What?"

"They arrested Tori. Was she behind all this?" I asked.

"Apparently. Andy was just about to fill me in – he's outside, and would like to see you."

"He is?" I said, sounding obviously surprised.

"I'm worried you're beginning to like Andy more than me," Melissa said in a somewhat serious tone. "Do you want him to come in?"

"Sure," I said. "I'd like to know what the hell's been going on." Melissa went to the entrance of the tent and leaned out. Always a man, my eyes locked onto the incredible shape of her butt as she put her head out. I knew I could never get tired of that. The lock on my gaze broke as she moved back to give Andy space to enter.

"Hello, Dan."   Hello *Dan?* This was impressive. "How are you feeling?"

"A little queasy, but okay," I replied, honestly. "I am dying to know what's going on, what with them arresting Tori and all. Was she the one trying to kill you?"   Andy paused a moment, then spoke,

"I guess the answer to that question is just *yes*. The Wood brothers were obviously the ones trying to kill me, but she was the reason. They caught Tommy Wood, and he spilled everything, implicating Tori, and so the Mounties came to get her.

"And the reason?" Melissa asked.

"That spec house we were in on together. Tori and I split the up front cost, and were to get 45 percent each, with the Woods getting ten percent plus being paid to build the house. I had just won a big check and needed to invest it to lessen the tax hit. To make a long story short, I gave Tori my money – "

Melissa interjected. "But she never passed it on to the Woods."

"Well, she did, but said it was her payment. I was away, and every time the Woods came after her for the rest she was telling them I was reneging on the deal. Then there was something about partner insurance, which I didn't even know about, and she convinced them they could get me back *and* collect the insurance by killing me."

"That doesn't sound like the brightest plan," I noted.

"We are not talking about the brightest people on the planet," Melissa rightly pointed out.

"Aren't I lucky that all this came to a boiling point the week I visit Heaven," I bemoaned.

"Well, you are a piece of the puzzle," Andy started. "When Tori and her pals got paired with you guys in the pro-am, Tori called me in Seattle and told me Melissa was back and with some guy, to draw me back to Heaven."

"And it worked," I said.

"Guess so. I am sorry."

"I'm sorry too," I replied.

"*You're* sorry? What on earth for?"

"For getting blood on your clubs."

"Oh hell, makes for a great war story. Though I'm not sure I want them back," Andy said with a smile. "Plus, you will need them for Alberta. That was quite the feat you pulled off on eighteen, by the way. Hitting those shots one-handed. Not sure I could have done that in the heat of battle."

"I'm sure you could," I said. "You're Andy Jones."

"Big dumb Andy Jones," Andy said.

"No," I replied.

"Yes," Melissa chimed in, just before the screaming started. It was clearly panicked screaming, outside and in the vicinity of the tent we were in. A shot rang out. Not a golf shot; the golf was over. A gun shot. Brian Wood burst into the medical tent with a forty-five. He raised it and pointed.

"Jones!" he shouted. And fired.

Andy dove to the ground. The echoes of Wood's shot had not yet cleared the air when two more shots followed rapidly. Red splattered on the white walls of the medical tent, then smeared by Brian Wood's slumping body as two Mounties burst in. I heard Melissa's voice, "Oh no!" I immediately looked down at Andy, laying on the grassy ground at my feet. He turned to look at me, seemingly okay, and then echoed Melissa's words,

"Oh no."

I looked down at my shirt. I had cheesily worn Tiger Woods' championship red that day. I put my hand to my chest and felt... nothing. With both hands I patted myself down, and felt nothing. I turned to look at Melissa, still standing on the other side of the cot I had been lying on. She just looked back at me with a blank expression. I noticed a red circular blotch on her pure white shirt. Just above her left breast. The blotch was growing in circumference, and suddenly she fell to her knees, and collapsed completely to the ground. I leapt over the cot and pulled Melissa onto my lap. Her shirt was now half covered in red as I stroked her blonde hair away from her lovely face. She looked at me, and then her eyes closed.

I screamed a scream that could be heard the other side of the golf course.

Chapter ~~69~~ 25

Melissa's house seemed so big, and so quiet. I had only been there a short while and yet I felt sentimental about every room we had been in. Especially the kitchen. I went into the kitchen, and stood in the middle. I sat right down in the center of the floor, and slid over to slump against the kitchen cupboards. I was sitting at the precise spot, the exact cupboard, where I had been sitting with Melissa, her leg swung over mine, after the first time we made love. My phone rang.

"Hello? Oh hi Andy. I'm okay. I'm at your house actually, just been collecting up some of Melissa's things. Ya, the realtor was by this morning, put the sign up. No problem. I know. I know you would. No, I don't know when I'll play again. I'll just have to see how I feel. Ya, I'm going there now. I know, I know you would. You just play well, okay? I will. Take care." I dropped the phone in my lap and stared out the window a moment.

I got to my feet, and meandered out to my car. My Corolla. I slowly drove down the mountain. Down the same road we had nearly all died on. It was such a long road, I had not noticed before. Finally I arrived at the main street, and turned right. Despite my lack of rush I was still early, and yet as I pulled into the main drive of the hospital my eye was immediately drawn to a nurse – an attractive one, I have to admit – pushing a wheelchair out the main doors. Melissa saw my car and her face lit up. Her beautiful, gorgeous, sweet face. I was in Heaven, after all.

The End

Acknowledgements

I would like to thank – in random order so no one is offended – V.Y., A.H., J.M., S.M., L.H., C.S., and W.S. for your support while writing this book. It is more appreciated than you know.
John Westley

About the Author

John Westley is originally from Portland, Oregon and currently lives a very private life in Vancouver, British Columbia. A former golf professional, he has been writing in various formats for many years and still finds time for the occasional round of golf. 69 Shades of Green (7 Days in Heaven) is his first novel, and he is currently working on the sequel. He can be reached via Facebook at
https://www.facebook.com/john.westley.332

Other Books from Thornhill Press
www.thornhillpress.com

Mystic Links (golf > fiction > short stories)
9 golf-themed short stories that mystically link the interesting characters involved in this crazy game.

Thumbs Down (golf > instruction)
The answer to learning to hit the golf ball solidly is as close as the thumbs on your hands!

Hit Down Dammit! (golf > instruction)
The single most common denominator in a struggling golf swing is a failure to understand the need to hit down at the golf ball. Hit Down Dammit! explains the concept and technique of hitting down at the golf ball for vastly improved ball striking.

Swing Issues (golf > instruction)
A collection of faults'n'fixes articles on almost every aspect of the swing imaginable.

Apron Strings & Family Ties (nonfiction > cookbook)
What started as Melody Gray's project of preserving a history of her family's wonderful recipes turned into a tremendous cookbook for all to enjoy.

Made in the USA
Charleston, SC
23 August 2014